Jealous Hearted...An Obsession for Love

Dominique Thomas

Jealous Hearted...An Obsession for Love

Text Shan to 22828 to stay up to date with new releases, sneak peeks, contest, and more…

Check your spam if you don't receive an email thanking you for signing up.

Text SPROMANCE to 22828 to stay up to date on new releases, plus get information on contest, sneak peeks, and more!

Table of Contents

Prologue

"Wait she's coming," the giggling teenage girl whispered.

Darby walked into the girl's room with her head hung low. She was fatigued, hungry, and sadly *stinking*. Her mother only allowed her to take one bath a week, and well, it just wasn't enough for the active young lady.

"Ugh, I can smell that fishy bitch," one of the cheerleaders griped. A few of the senior cheerleaders, who happened to be on the varsity team, shook their heads in disapproval at the scene before them.

Darby walked by the group of girls as they jumped from behind the lockers and started spraying her with deodorant and throwing soap bars at her. She instantly started crying and shielding her face from the chaos.

"Bitch, you stink!"

"Dirty Darby!" Another one chanted. They all laughed.

"Dirty Darby. Dirty Darby," they repeated over and over again.

Darby fell onto the floor and curled into a ball. She cried until the girls ran off. Lourdes walked into the locker room with her best friend, Sundae, and they looked down at Darby as she lay on the floor crying. They both dropped down to their knees to check on her.

"Oh my god, are you okay?" Lourdes asked on the verge of tears herself.

Darby shook her head too embarrassed to even look at the girls. Sundae stood up and ran off to get some help while Lourdes soothingly rubbed Darby's back. She'd seen the girl before and felt so bad at how her fellow classmates often treated her.

"It's okay, Darby. Fuck them bitches," she said wishing she could have shielded Darby from the pain and embarrassment.

"No, it's okay," Darby sniffled and wiped her eyes.

Sundae walked back up with the gym teacher. The gym teacher looked at the mess before her and sighed. She was so tired of all of the girls picking on Darby, but still there was nothing she could do. The kids that bullied Darby were what you would call special students. Their parents did stuff like donate thousands to the school and helped build new wings in the school. There was no way the principle would let her discipline the students that were involved.

"Darby, come on, dear. Go take a shower while I talk with Lourdes and Sundae," she said helping Darby stand. Darby used her time at school to eat and shower.

"Okay," Darby said and walked off leaving a scent of fish behind in her wake.

The ladies pretended not to smell it. The gym teacher, Miss Nancy, looked at Lourdes and Sundae. Lourdes' parents were wealthy. They both were lawyers and lived a good life. She knew that if Lourdes was to complain it would get noticed before her saying something.

"Lourdes, I need to ask you something. Will you tell the principal about what you walked in on?" Miss Nancy asked with hopeful eyes. Lourdes and Sundae both nodded immediately. Sundae also had clout, because her father was a big time judge.

"Yes we both will," Sundae said. Miss Nancy was so happy that she cried.

"Thank God! Please go do that now, and I'll find Darby clean clothes to put on." Lourdes stopped smiling to look at Miss Nancy. She hated that Darby was getting put through so many changes.

"Miss Nancy, Sundae and I can bring her a whole bin of clothes tomorrow with fresh deodorant." Miss Nancy smiled appreciatively.

"Lourdes, baby, that would be heaven sent. Please do that and God bless you two," she said before walking off.

Lourdes and Sundae practically ran to the principal's office. They were immediately seen and they began to tell the principal about what they believed happened to Darby. He watched them with an indifferent look on his handsome, olive-colored face. He had more important things to handle like the school's concert that was coming up, or his trip to the Cayman Islands that he was due to take in just a few short weeks.

"Listen, girls. This is an isolated incident. I promise you I will get down to the bottom of it," he said and they both smiled. They were green to the ways of the world. At the moment they believed him.

In the following days life changed drastically for Darby. Lourdes and Sundae took her under their wing. They clothed her as if she was their own child, and even picked her up in Lourdes' new red Mustang she'd gotten for her sixteenth birthday. Darby for once in her life felt special. People were afraid to go against her now that she was friends with Lourdes and Sundae. They didn't like her, but they also didn't pick on her anymore.

However, Darby was still living in hell at home. What Darby didn't know was that her mother only wanted sons. Her mother's life had consisted of women hating on her because of her beauty. It made her start to hate them so much so that she had no female friends. She also didn't trust them and Darby was no different. Diana didn't want any women around her husband, not even a daughter that she had created with him.

"I hope you don't think you cute now, Darby. All you look like is a damn wanna be," Diana said and blew cigarette smoke from her pouty lips. Secretly she was jealous of how well Darby cleaned up, and how much better Darby's sixteen-year-old body looked compared to her forty-year-old frame.

Darby ignored her mother and she continued to walk towards her bedroom. She stepped into her room as her father came out of the bathroom. He looked at her in clothes that he thought his wife had bought and he smiled.

"Hi, princess, come give daddy a hug," he said.

Darby cringed. It wasn't because her father was a pervert or anything. She knew that the simple gesture of love would piss her mother off. Darby shook her head and clutched down onto her stomach.

"Daddy, my stomach is cramping. I just wanna lay down," she faked. Her father nodded.

"Okay, baby girl, try to get you some rest. I put some money on your dresser so that you could do something over the weekend with your new friends. I love you, honey," he said.

Darby started to cry with her back now turned to him. "I love you too, Daddy," she said and closed her bedroom door.

Darby stripped out of her clothes and laid down in her bed to take a nap. As she was starting to dose off, she could hear her bedroom door creak open. She pulled the covers over her head fearing the worst.

"I swear you are so ungrateful. I do so much for you, Darby, and this is how you do me. Got him giving you money and shit. I'm his wife! He belongs to me," Diana hissed and slapped Darby in the back of her head with her hand as hard as she could. Darby covered her mouth to muffle her cries.

"Dumb bitch. I swear the minute you turn eighteen you getting the fuck up from out of here. Only queen bee in this house is me. Stupid ass little girl," she said and snatched the $100 bill off of the dresser.

Diana walked back out of the room and Darby cried herself to sleep. That weekend Darby ended up hanging out with Lourdes and Sundae and some boys. Darby was beyond nervous, because she secretly crushed on Lourdes' boyfriend Qwote. He was the star of the football team and, in Darby's eyes, perfect.

The teenagers all sat in Lourdes' house that was like a mansion to Darby. Lourdes', parents were out of town, and she was doing what most teens did when they had the chance. She was partying.

"Aye who this?" Qwote asked walking into the room.

Darby held her head down as she felt all of the eyes in the room zero in on her. Lourdes had flat ironed her hair and given her a cute tube dress to put on. Darby felt cute until she went around Lourdes and Sundae. They really were in a league of their own. They held an air of confidence in them that she just didn't possess.

"That's Darby and be nice, Qwote," Lourdes said before taking a sip of her drink.

Qwote looked Darby over and shook his head. Lourdes was always trying to save someone. He wasn't surprised at all to see she had picked up a stray and brought her into their circle. Qwote sat down onto the sofa and started to roll up a blunt.

"Darby, what's good? Where did our girl Lolo find you at?" he asked.

Lourdes gave Qwote a look and he smirked at her. Darby slowly looked up and she could feel the air leave her body. Qwote was everything that she ever wanted in a boyfriend. He had light caramel colored skin with slanted brown eyes, and full brown lips that were outlined by a thin mustache. His hair was cut low and waved up giving him a look of a mixed descent because of the silky texture of his hair. Qwote was still in high school, but he held an array of tattoos that Darby swooned over; including the one he had on his hand that was a rose with his mother's name inside of it.

It was the way Qwote handled himself that turned Darby on the most. His presence was commanding, and he was always the center of attention. Like now, all eyes were on him including Darby's. She was incredibly jealous of Lourdes for having such a sexy boyfriend.

"I go to school with y'all," she said nervously.

Qwote nodded his head as he continued to break down his blunt. He had never seen Darby a day in his life, and he felt like he knew everyone. His brother Quamir stepped into the room followed by a disheveled Sundae. They walked over to the loveseat and sat down.

"Quamir, you know who this is?" Qwote asked him.

Quamir sat up as Sundae tried to lay all over him. He squinted his chestnut colored eyes as he stared at Darby. He chuckled and sat back. Sundae whispered something in his ear and gave him a stern look.

"Yeah, she goes to school with us. This is dirt—Darby," he corrected after Sundae hit his arm.

Darby looked at Quamir and rolled her eyes. She had crushed on him as well, but Quamir was rude most of the time and gave no fucks about anyone's feelings except Sundae's. Darby liked that Qwote gave everyone an equal amount of respect.

Qwote lit up his blunt and took a few hits even blowing the smoke in Lourdes' face making her mad. He looked at Darby and gave her a wink.

"Welcome to the crew, ma," he said and Darby could feel butterflies form in the pit of her stomach.

Darby spent a beautiful summer with Lourdes and Sundae. They all did everything together and Darby ended up losing her virginity to one of Qwote's friends Issa. School quickly started and Darby had a school year with limited bullying and even a boyfriend. She praised her good school life to Lourdes and Sundae. They all went to prom together and graduated together as well.

Darby sadly had to say goodbye to her friends over the summer as they left Detroit for college in New York. She wasn't accepted to the school that they were attending, because of her mother she didn't receive the proper financial aid. While Lourdes and Sundae prepared for a new life, Darby was kicked out by her mother and homeless. She began a quick descend to the bottom that made her grow hatred for the very people who claimed to love her including Sundae and Lourdes.

Chapter One

Present day

"No, baby, I can't," Lourdes whined while gripping the sheets. Qwote shook his head as he continued to slowly slide in and out of her.

"Nah, you was talking mad shit over the phone. You knew the minute a nigga touched down I was gonna tear that pussy up. Stop playing and open your fucking legs," he said with a devilish grin on his face.

Lourdes' eyes rolled into the back of her head. She opened her legs as wide as she could, and Qwote as promised commenced to fucking the shit out of her. She could only stare up at him with a sexy fuck face as he tore her walls down. Legs high up in the air with the room smelling of their sexual escapade, Lourdes began to cum. Her body tingled, and she knew that without a doubt nobody would ever fuck her like Qwote did.

"Oh, baaabbbyyy. Right fucking there!" she panted.

Qwote licked his full lips and bent down to give Lourdes a sensual kiss that dug so deep into him that he started to cum. He quickly pulled out and let off on her stomach. Qwote fell down beside Lourdes and breathed hard to catch his breath. He and Lourdes had been fucking for hours trying to christen their new condo. They were in the process of building a home but the home had, at least, another year on it. They had to lease a place because Lourdes was back from New York and didn't wanna stay in Qwote's loft.

"Damn, ma, that shit was good," he said and looked over at her.

Lourdes was breathing hard as well. She was also still reeling from her climax. She slowly sat up and Qwote kissed her arm. She gave him a warm smile until she felt his warm cum slide into her belly button. She frowned at the feel of it. Qwote picked up on it and got out of the bed.

"Aye, you just got home. We in a good space so don't come at me with that bullshit, Lourdes," he warned her as he walked into the connecting bathroom. Lourdes watched Qwote walk back into the room minutes later with a wet ivory washcloth. He washed her stomach and in between her legs.

"With what bullshit, Quinton?" she asked using his real name.

Qwote looked up at her with his slanted eyes and he smirked. After ten years of being with Lourdes, she was still the only woman that he ever loved. The only woman that ever got away with whatever. She was his baby. The reason he grinded so hard. The reason why he was building an expensive ass house far away from his boys and his business. It was all because of her.

"Bae, you know what. When the time is right for a kid we will have one. We not even married right now, so don't start with that 'when you gon' give me a baby shit'," he replied and walked off.

Lourdes was so upset she fell back onto the bed and crossed her arms over her big breasts. She hated when Qwote pissed her off then made himself impossible to be mad at. As much as he loved her she loved him. Qwote had sampled a few women, in the beginning, stages of their relationship but Lourdes had only been with him. Well there was a little situation with another guy, but that was one secret she would gladly take to her grave. That type of secret could bring down the love she had with Qwote in an instant.

Qwote was handsome on most days. Fine as hell every day. Thugged out on the weekends, and one fine ass man in a suit Monday through Friday. Lourdes loved Qwote so much that it bordered on worshipping him. He was sweet with her. He loved her. He took care of her needs even while she was away in New York attending school. Never once did she ever have to wonder what he was doing. He was that much of a good man to her. Lourdes would bet her savings on him and knew that she would double or triple her profit. Qwote was that much of a sure thing, only his beliefs weren't cohesive with hers anymore.

Qwote was in his prime. Twenty-six, and running a successful investment firm. Qwote and his friends were all young, black, successful men and to a lot of women that was a rarity that they weren't drug dealers. Qwote didn't have baby momma drama or a rap sheet. All he had was stocks and bonds. A 401k plan with cd's and shit. He had a plan to be a millionaire before he turned thirty then he would marry Lourdes and pump her with as many kids as she wanted. Until then he was enjoying his woman being back home after spending six years away from him in New York.

He wanted to spoil and fuck her and all she seemed to want to do was bitch at him. He didn't get it.

"*Mi Amor*, come here," he said patting his lap.

Lourdes licked her suddenly dry lips. She wanted to deny him but she couldn't. She rolled her eyes frustrated at the power he had over her. Qwote chuckled while looking at her. He knew that she could never deny him when he called her *my love* which she was. She crawled over onto his lap and gazed down at him. Lourdes was gorgeous. Her beauty wasn't over exaggerated. She was a classic beauty. Chocolate brown skin with short, cropped hair and high cheekbones. Lourdes had wide hips with a nice size ass that kept Qwote rubbing and licking on it. He loved everything about her including her natural beauty. The pucker of her lips. The dimples in her cheeks when she smiled and the sexiness of her body when she was and wasn't clothed. Lourdes was and would always be the shit to him as he was to her.

Qwote had dark brown eyes, light caramel colored skin, and full lips that were outlined with a thin mustache. He had thick, silky hair the color of coal that was cut low to his head in an array of waves. Qwote *always* had a fresh line up. He wasn't a pretty boy, but cared very much about his looks and maintained them well. He stayed groomed for himself and for Lourdes as well.

He had thick brows that had shaped themselves into a natural curve that wasn't womanly, but just a nice groomed brow. He had slanted eyes with a strong square jaw and long slender nose. He was tall standing at 6'5 and he was almost two hundred and sixty pounds of pure muscle. Qwote and his boys spent five days out of the week at the gym talking shit and working out their bodies. Qwote was built in all of the right places, and his workout did not take away from his thick, penis that stayed hard for Lourdes.

"Listen you're finally home. We been talking about this shit for years. Staying on the phone all hours of the night wishing we was here at this exact moment. Don't let what other people are doing fuck up what we have. I know Sundae is pregnant, and I know it hurt you but you should just be happy for her. When the time is right you will be pregnant too, bae. Your man's got a plan, and I'm not breaking it because of what other people feel we should be doing," he told her.

Lourdes sighed. "This is about what I want, Qwote. I want a baby," she whined and actually poked her lip out.

Qwote looked at her incredulously. "Aye, you real fucking spoiled and you acting kind of selfish. We should both want a child before we take that step. Are you not wifey material? You okay with being my baby momma?" he asked her.

"Of course not!"

Qwote smiled. "Then why you tripping? Only ring you wearing is my promise ring from the twelfth grade that I keep upgrading. You deserve the ring and the title way before you give me the baby. I know you didn't move back to the D so that you could be mad at me."

Lourdes looked away from him and she shook her head. Qwote had a way of turning a situation around and making her feel like she was always the one in the wrong.

"Qwote, you know I didn't want that. I love you, and I'm happy that I'm back home with you for good," she said staring back down at him.

Qwote eyed her then her breasts. He licked his lips while palming her ass. "Then show daddy just how happy you are to be home with him," he said and Lourdes bent down to kiss him.

The next day Lourdes woke up to a note and breakfast in bed on a tray. She knew that if people saw Qwote they would never guess that he was so romantic and sweet but he was. She smiled lazily and rubbed the sleep away from her eyes. Lourdes grabbed the note and read it.

Aye, mi amor, daddy did not wanna leave your beautiful ass in bed, but I had no choice. I gotta get to the money. I have a meeting in Ann Arbor today, but I will be back in time to help your pops move your shit in. I'll bring Quamir with me. Look I know last night you said you was good, but I could see you was hurt. Bae, I love you. I only wanna better myself for you. Don't ever think your best interests are not in my heart. I love your ass girl. Keep that thang wet for me...

Lourdes smiled and looked at her tray. She pulled the cover back and was graced with pancakes and cheese eggs. She sat up and prayed before scarfing down the food quickly. She grabbed her phone and sent Qwote an "I love you" text before getting out of the bed and using the bathroom. After showering and brushing her teeth, Lourdes began to unpack her boxes. She'd spent six years in New York working at her social worker's degree and now she finally had it. She felt so accomplished yet she knew her life was just now beginning. She knew she was still young, so she did feel wrong about pressuring Qwote for kids, but it was hard when she talked to Sundae and could hear the excitement in her voice. Sundae was married to a New York but Detroit-born music producer, and she was expecting their first child. Lourdes would never admit it but for the first time in her life, she was actually jealous of someone.

It seemed like Sundae was living the life while Lourdes felt like she and Qwote had kind of hit a road block, because shit with them was just the *same*. The sex was still great and thankfully the excitement was still there, but they didn't have a baby to look forward to.

"Well, at least, he's giving me a house," she pacified herself as she grabbed some boxes.

Hours flew by and Lourdes found herself halfway through unpacking her bedroom. The condo was two bedrooms and two baths and it was actually pretty big with it being over 2,000 square feet. She was happy with what Qwote had chosen for them. The ringing doorbell got her attention. Lourdes rushed to the door and smiled wide when she saw it was her father and uncle. Lourdes was an only child, so her family often treated her like royalty. That was one of the many reasons why they had given her such a unique name. She was everything to her parents.

"Hey, baby girl," Randy said hugging his daughter.

Lourdes hugged her father then her uncle, who happened to be the chief of police. She welcomed them into her condo and was about to shut the door until someone caught her eye. Lourdes walked outside and spotted a gorgeous woman getting out of a brand new, royal blue Mercedes-AMG coupe. The woman looked to be around her age. The woman also looked like she could have been a Victoria's Secrets model with her to die for body. She looked up at Lourdes and stared at her.

The stare was so intense yet so familiar. Lourdes found herself stepping back into the house and closing the door. She wasn't sure why but an uneasiness feeling swept over her. She walked into her living room and found her father and uncle watching ESPN and drinking Qwote's Coronas. She smiled at the scene before her.

"Princess, you know you could have moved to the condo in Farmington Hills that we got you," her father said.

Lourdes looked at her dad with nothing but love and adoration in her heart for him. He'd shown her what it was like to be properly loved by a man, so she knew that she lucked up when she got Qwote because he was one of a kind.

"I know, Dad, and I appreciate all that you and Mom do for me, but I want to live with Qwote. You know he's getting the house built for us, and I thought this year could warm us up to living together."

"I'm happy for you two also. Quinton is a good man. He was just on the news last week for donating money to the shelter in the city. I swear these young black men need to look up to him. I'm just ready for him to make an honest woman out of my baby," Randy said and looked at her.

Lourdes smiled at him. "And he will, Daddy. I can assure you of that," she said flashing him her promise ring that was more expensive than some women's engagement rings.

"I know he will. Your moving truck should be here soon, so we will relax until then," he said and Lourdes found a seat next to her father. Like he'd predicted the truck soon came and Qwote came home in time for him to help them move Lourdes' stuff into their place. Lourdes was tired but thankful to be finally back in Detroit for good.

Chapter Two

Darby sat inside of her living room on the floor with three lines of coke in front of her. She'd already done two lines and was contemplating if she should do more. Seeing Lourdes had been fucking with her all week. Seeing the beautiful, chocolate skinned beauty took her back to her high school days. She hated thinking of the past. Those days were behind her. Now she got any man she wanted, and they paid any price to be with her.

A hoe she was not; neither was she a prostitute. She was a high-priced escort that gave men a good time for a lot of money. She adored her men because they afforded her the life she was living. She was even fucking three of the cheerleaders', who bullied her in high school, husbands for free just to get payback. Darby had done much worse than that, so she felt she was taking it lightly on them. For the principal in high school that wouldn't help her, she'd gotten him back really good and was still getting him back. For her mother well... all she would say about that was karma was truly a bitch.

Darby decided to sniff the lines and before she knew it she was wired. She couldn't sit still she was so damn high. She cut on some music and started dancing to the beat as she smiled over how gorgeous Lourdes was. Darby had been admiring

Qwote secretly for weeks since he had moved in and was looking for a chance to make her move. She had no idea he was still with Lourdes until she saw her outside of the condo staring directly at her.

"She didn't know! Ha!" Darby laughed. She started to laugh so hard she bent over almost peeing on herself. "The bitch didn't know who I was! Thank you, Doctor Mallory! My nigga, my nigga!" she shouted, proud that her $20,000 makeover was well worth the pain, money, and time.

Darby now had full Double-D cup breasts, a small waist with a bubble implanted butt. She had a fake nose, collagen-infused lips with cheek implants and a raised hairline. To the eye, she looked amazing. Her doctor was amazing at what he did. She didn't look crazy and her work was befitting of her 5'7 frame. She could easily be a model or even Miss America yet she had chosen to be nothing more than a high-priced escort. All of the money in the world couldn't fix the low self-esteem she had. Darby didn't love herself, so she had no clue just how precious her body was. She gave it away for a price and somehow that made her feel like she was somebody. Hell all her life people had been telling her she was no one. Now she had a condo that was paid for with two Mercedes, and over a $100,000 in the bank.

"I'm definitely not a lame bitch now," she said while sitting down onto the floor.

Darby pulled out her cell and looked Lourdes up on Facebook. She found her almost instantly and sent her a friend request, she then started to look through her photos. Darby smiled at all of the pictures wishing she could have seen those places with Lourdes. She even kissed a few of the pics that had Qwote's fine ass in them.

Darby stopped on a picture of Lourdes and Sundae and she started to cry. She'd loved them for so long, and she hated them for leaving her. They selfishly went off to college while she was left to fend for herself.

"Those bitches didn't care about me. I was living on the street until Kirk found me. Stupid ass, spoiled ass hoes," she said angrily.

She narrowed her eyes at the pictures of the two women in Vegas, just a few short months ago, living it up.

"Oh, my name Lourdes and I think I'm sooooo cute. Hmph well, my name is Sundae and bitch my man produce whack ass songs that never make it to the radio. We balling, bitch!" she said sarcastically mimicking the girls.

Darby rolled her eyes and tossed her phone across the room. She hated them hoes for forgetting about her.

"That's alright because I got something for they asses. Stupid ass bitches," she said as she slipped her hand between her slim thighs. She closed her eyes and licked her plump lips.

"Mmmm, Qwote," she moaned while circling her clitoris with her thumb. "I want you to fuck me, daddy," she moaned.

Darby slipped two fingers inside of herself and she cried out. She could actually envision Qwote's big body hovering over hers as he slowly entered her. She pictured him looking down at her with his enchanting eyes and smiling wickedly.

"That bitch don't feel as good as you," he would tell her while rocking his dick in and out of her. Darby cried out thinking it was real.

"I know she don't! With them fat ass hips she can't possibly fuck you as good as me. Please, Qwote, beat this pussy up," she begged before climaxing all on her fingers.

Darby moaned and laid on her floor for a moment to gain her composure. She smiled then started to laugh.

"Ohhh I can't wait to fuck him!" she said excitedly before jumping up. Darby's cell phone started to ring and she checked the ID. She laughed again. She just loved how the tides had finally turned in her favor.

"What do you want?" she answered while licking her arousal off of her fingers.

"Darby…please you know I need it. Your brother won't take my calls. Can you bring that to momma, baby?" her mother asked. Darby smiled. It was a wicked grin that made her look almost demonic.

"Why, Mother dear. You must know there isn't nothing I wouldn't do for you," she said and ended the call. Darby slipped on her pants and grabbed her purse. She took her good coke out and sat it on her dining room table. She then picked up the cheap crack and put it in her newest Louie bag. She grabbed her car keys and exited her house, so that she could give her mother a fix. On some days, she made Diana trick for the crack money, but because she was in a good mood she decided to give her some on credit. After all what were daughter's for if they couldn't help out a parent in need?

Chapter Three

"So how is work coming along?"

Lourdes rubbed Sundae's stomach and smiled at her. Yes, she was envious of her because she wanted a child, but still she was happy for her best friend.

"It's cool. The people are not nice to me, though. The women all look at me like I took their fucking man, and well the men all look at my ass. I'm taking it day to day. Qwote threatened to go up there and slap a few of them bitches for me, but I told him no. I wanted this job and now that I have it, I just have to deal with it. But guess what?"

Sundae turned her bright eyes to Lourdes. "What?"

"Why did Darby send me a friend request," Lourdes said excitedly.

Sundae's face lit up as well. "What? Bitch, you lying," she said and Lourdes laughed.

"No, I'm serious. I've been messaging her and come to find out she stays next door to me. I had actually saw her, but I didn't know who she was. She looks…different now," Lourdes said thinking back on Darby's new look.

Sundae rubbed her eyes. She was tired already and they had only been out for a few hours. "Different how?"

"Well from what I saw she now has breast implants and her face done. It looks very different now. Like on some real shit she looks like one of those black Hawaiian Barbie dolls that be at Target for $10. I invited her over tonight for drinks. When you see her, bitch, please don't stare," she replied.

Sundae laughed. "Now I'ma stare just because you asked me not to. I did miss the hell out of Darby, though. She was really cool once we got her to open herself up to us," Sundae said.

Lourdes nodded. She felt the exact same way. "I know. I looked through her pics and her ass travels more than we do. She seems the same, and I'm excited to be linking up with her."

"Yeah me too. So how are things with you and Qwote?"

Lourdes blushed just from thinking about her man. "We're good. I'm still upset about the baby and marriage thing, but I'm being patient. I know I have a good man."

"You do so don't lose him because of some bullshit. I already told you now that you home this will be our kid. Drama just linked up with a lot of music people here, so he's actually good with us moving back, plus he has his family and stuff. Our niggas aren't necessarily friends but they about to be," Sundae said and they both laughed.

Sundae had dated Qwote's brother for three years before she met Drama at a club in New York one night. Drama became the side nigga that ended up being her husband. Qwote's brother hated Drama and everything he stood for, because he had in fact stolen his woman and now he was about to have a baby with her. Drama, however, gave no fucks. Sundae was his dream woman, and he would never regret getting with her.

"Well Quamir is always over there, so Drama will never be welcome, but I will talk to Qwote and let him know that Drama is your husband. They just going to have to get over the bullshit. I'm home and I'm not letting that get in the way of our friendship," Lourdes said and Sundae blew her a kiss.

"My girl," she said and they finished the rest of their lunch.

Later that day while Sundae, Drama, and Qwote watched a movie Lourdes made drinks. She was anxious to see Darby. The tension in the condo was already thick because Qwote and Drama refused to even talk to each other. Lourdes was tired of the childish behavior and two seconds away from telling both of them grown ass men off.

"Two grown ass men sitting on opposite ends of the couch frowning at each other. Shit is silly," she said while pouring herself a glass of wine.

"Who you in here talking about?" Qwote asked sneaking up on her.

Lourdes laughed and smiled back at him. She was upset with how he was acting, but that still didn't take away from the fact that he was looking edible in his black dress shirt that was unbuttoned at the collar with his black slacks on. She knew that tomorrow he would be in jeans and Timbs, and damn a versatile nigga was so sexy to her.

"Nothing, daddy," she said and went back to her drinks.

Qwote knew she was lying, but he chuckled and walked up on her. He wrapped his arms around her waist and started kissing on her soft neck.

"That ass getting bigger, Lourdes. You gon' let me put something up in it?" he asked poking his erection into her.

Lourdes moaned while sipping her drink. "Qwote…that feel funny to me. Like I gotta take a shit," she said and he roared with laughter.

"Ma, that's because you always so tense. I'ma make sure it's good and wet…come on," he begged while groping her and sticking his long tongue in her ear.

Lourdes' head fell back against him and a throat cleared from behind them.

They both turned around and were face to face with a barely dressed Darby. Qwote didn't want to, but his dick got even harder at what she had on. It was a white shirt with no bra exposing her pierced nipples with stone wash, skinny jeans that were so tight they were exposing her fat camel toe. He didn't remember this Darby at all, because if she would have looked anything like that in high school on everything she would have gotten fucked by him.

He stepped to the side and allowed for Lourdes to walk over to Darby.

"Girl, you look good! Come here!" she yelled and Darby walked up on her.

Darby hugged Lourdes hard while making sure she kept eye contact with Qwote. Her stare was so intense he had to turn away and grab his blunt wraps. It was Thursday night. He had no meetings tomorrow, so he was about to get good and lifted.

"What up, Darby. You looking good, girl," he told her before quickly exiting the room.

"You too," Darby said pulling back from Lourdes

Damn that bitch was hugging the fuck out of me, Darby thought smiling at Lourdes.

Lourdes gave Darby a once over and was pleased. Darby looked good, he pictures did her no justice. She grabbed Darby's hand and pulled her into the back of the condo. Lourdes handed Darby a soft cardigan while smiling at her.

"I still love you like a sister, but you will not be around my nigga with them big ass titties exposed like that," she said seriously.

Bitch. Darby wanted to say but instead, she laughed it off, and put on the thin sweater that matched her outfit. They walked out of the room and grabbed the drinks before joining everyone in the living room. Qwote was rolling up a blunt while Drama looked at his phone, and Sundae was stretched out beside him on the loveseat.

"We're all back together again!" Lourdes said excitedly and clapped.

Darby and Sundae giggled. Lourdes had always been the extra happy one of the group. Sundae looked at Darby and she smiled. She was impressed with the work Darby had done, because Darby looked gorgeous. Darby too stared at

Sundae. She hated to see that Sundae was still beautiful as ever with her bright eyes and flawless brown skin. Sundae had always gotten attention because of her wide eyes that were colored funny. Darby hated her for that too. *This bitch still looks like a mutt*, she thought.

"Sundae, that baby is going to have those beautiful eyes, girl. How many months are you?" she asked. Sundae rubbed her stomach.

"Six. How have you been? Bitch, you look like you living good," Sundae said admiring Darby's different colored diamond bangles and earrings that she knew cost a grip.

"I've been doing me. I'm in sales for this company, and well I manage to get by. I missed you two so much. For years I prayed that I would see y'all again. I even searched for y'all on the internet and shit like a stalker," she said jokingly, but she was dead ass serious.

Lourdes and Sundae laughed thinking she was joking. "I know I just put my Facebook page back up, but I'm back and you're back as well. I'm excited!" Lourdes said excitedly.

Sundae and Darby laughed while Qwote side eyed her. "I'ma have to give your happy ass some of this weed. Shit, your cheering days are over, ma," he said and smiled at her.

Lourdes scrunched up her face at him and he chuckled. "*Mi amor,* give daddy a kiss," he demanded.

Lourdes happily obeyed and leaned over to give him a sensual kiss on the lips. Darby watched the encounter so turned on she actually rubbed her thighs together.

Damn, I can't wait to fuck this fine ass nigga, she thought staring at them. No one picked up on her stare, because Sundae was wrapped up in her husband. For the next two hours, the women caught up on what they had been doing then eventually Darby left. For once since he had been there Drama spoke. He looked at Sundae then Lourdes. He wasn't sure if he was right, but he knew about Darby from one of his friends.

"Aye I think I know her,'" he said.

"How?" Sundae asked immediately going into defense mode.

Drama and Qwote both chuckled. "Not like that, bae. I mean it could be or couldn't be her. My nigga, B, that I did some songs for, was talking about this chick that he fucked on a regular for money and shit. He was showing pics of her body and the bitch was stacked. She looked just like old girl, but honestly that was a while ago, and we were all fucked up," he said realizing he could have been very wrong about Darby.

"Yeah, Darby would never trick. She doesn't have to do any nasty shit like that," Lourdes said and Sundae nodded agreeing with her.

"Yeah she's not that kind of woman," Sundae cosigned.

Drama made eye contact with Qwote and they both smiled at how naive women could be.

"Well y'all haven't seen her in years so don't act like y'all fucking know that girl. And shit you never know what a motherfucka would do for that paper," Qwote said standing up. He pulled some money out of his pocket and rained it all over Lourdes. "I mean what you willing to do for this?" he asked and she jumped up.

"Qwote, don't put no nasty ass money on me!" she snapped and hit his arm.

Qwote laughed and grabbed her hips. "Aye let y'all selves out when y'all ready. Lourdes gotta go earn that shoe money I just rained on her," he joked and pulled her away.

Sundae laughed as they walked away. Qwote took Lourdes into the bedroom and shut the door. He dropped her down onto the bed and she giggled. Just being in his presence made her so damn happy. She sat up and pulled her tank top off. She then undid her bra as Qwote stared down at her.

"Don't tease a nigga, get naked," he said and licked his lips.

Lourdes creamed at his words. She laid back and pulled off her slacks that had been hugging her ass all night. She pulled her thongs off with them and Qwote looked over her beautiful body. She was so perfect to him. Her breasts was big and perky and her ass, well shit, it needed some sort of reward for being so perfect. He bit down onto his bottom lip while staring at her.

"Play with that pussy and you better show her some love," he demanded.

Lourdes opened her legs and slowly slid her hand down her body. She slipped it between her juicy thighs and started to play with herself while staring into Qwote's eyes. Her breathing became labored as he gave her this intense gaze.

"Get her wet for me," he said in a thick, needy voice.

Lourdes moaned. She stuck two fingers inside of herself and pumped them in and out of her vagina. Qwote unbuttoned his shirt and took it off. He tossed it onto the floor and slowly walked over to the bed. Lourdes stopped and he frowned at her.

"Don't stop. Get that shit," he said and grabbed her leg. Qwote pulled her towards him and he began to suck on her toes while she fingered herself. After a few minutes, he looked down at his woman.

"Why you not cumming? I see you playing games with my shit tonight," he said and kissed his way down her leg and eventually between it. He kissed her vaginal lips sensually as if they were the lips on her mouth.

Lourdes moaned and arched her back. She grabbed his head and that shit drove him wild. He stuck his long tongue as deep into Lourdes as it would go. He fucked her with it for a few seconds before she started cumming all over it. Qwote didn't stop until his mouth and bottom of his face was drenched in her arousal. He flipped her over and unbuckled his pants. He'd wanted her ass earlier, but her pussy was so enticing he knew he had to have it instead.

"We can do anal another day. I gotta slide up in my shit," he said and slowly penetrated her.

"Oh shit! Qwote…. you feel so good, daddy. You feel so damn good inside of me," Lourdes said moaning loudly.

Qwote slapped her ass hard and grabbed her hips. "You do too, baby. I missed the fuck out of this pussy. I also missed the fuck out of you. Can you feel how much I did?" he asked and hit it so hard the bed shook.

Lourdes yelped. "I do! Oh! I do," she said with teary eyes.

Qwote massaged her ass before hitting it again. He repeated the process until Lourdes came all over his dick then he came all over her ass wishing he could cum inside of her. As he laid down so that she could ride him, he made up in his head she was getting on birth control. Now he just needed to convince her of that without it becoming another argument.

Chapter Four

"Here you go," Brandon said to Darby. Darby took the money and placed it in her satchel. She smiled at Brandon while he stared at her. "My homeboy asked me about you yesterday too."

"What?"

Brandon laughed at the way Darby's face fell. He low-key loved her because she was so nasty yet so classy with her shit, but he could never wife a whore. He sat back on the king sized bed and smiled at her.

"My nigga Drama asked me about you. I told him he had the wrong woman, but yeah somehow he saw some pics that you had sent me and shit. He was saying you went to school with his wife. I covered for you, though," he said almost in a way like she should have been grateful to him.

Darby moved like a cheetah as she leaped onto the bed and on top of Brandon. He was a cute, dark-skinned man that was a rapper, but his real job was hustling. He was young, rich, and reckless. She liked his money and that was it. She gave no fucks about ruining his life.

Darby clutched Brandon's balls tightly in her hand. She made sure to dig her stiletto nail deep into his ball sack. Brandon winced and grabbed a handful of her hair. They stared each other down neither refusing to let go.

"When I say I will ruin you, I'm not fucking playing. Don't you ever discuss what we do, Brandon. I swear you bragging ass, wanna be fly ass niggas irritate the fuck out of me. The niggas that gets pussy all day don't have to brag about it. Now I come when you call, because I make 10k every time. Don't think it's because of this little ass baby dick you got because it's not. I got your dick pics too. I can put that shit on the internet right now, and show these hoes you ain't worth their time. Try me," she warned and let him go.

Brandon punched her as hard as he could and she fell off the bed. Darby grabbed her face and Brandon jumped on top of her. He commenced to whipping her ass. She had not only squeezed the fuck out of his nut sack, but she had also hurt his ego. He knew he had a little dick. That was one of the reasons why he paid for sex. With working women, they didn't belittle him. They made him feel like the king he was. He fucked Darby up so bad she fell unconscious a few times. He shook her until she came to then put her in the hallway, naked, with the money for their sex in her purse that he placed beside her. He then spit on her face and went back into his hotel suite. He was quite certain Darby wouldn't retaliate. He'd given her the money, and he knew deep down that she only cared about that anyway.

Darby woke up in a hospital room hours later. She winced when she tried to look around.

"Who did you piss off this time?" Kirk asked.

Darby frowned at the sound of her old pimp's voice. Kirk, at one point in time, was her savior until she learned that like everyone else he didn't love her. He used her and often sold her for money or jewels, even drugs sometimes. He always went back for her, but he made her the whore she was. Through him, she met Daniella a madam and became a high-priced call girl. Kirk was upset that Darby had succeeded without him. Now that he had AIDS and was growing close with God, he was trying to save Darby before she faced the same fate as him.

"No one," she let out.

Kirk looked at all of her bruises and chuckled. "Well, that no one worked you over. Darby, you have to let this life go. It doesn't love you, baby girl. It doesn't love anyone. The devil is lying to you," he said pleading with her.

Darby rolled her eyes. She was *so* tired of the Jesus talk with Kirk. Damn he was driving her insane with it. She only took his calls because in a way she was connected to him. She hated and loved him at the same time. Her father had died years ago from lung cancer, and while Kirk could never be him, he was there for her at times.

"Kirk, please...I don't wanna hear this bullshit. I keep telling you God doesn't exist. If he did I wouldn't have had this fucked up life," she said.

Kirk dropped down to his knees. He prayed wherever he was at. Whenever the need washed over him he prayed.

"God, help her. She is still so blinded by the devil. He's convinced her that you don't love her, Lord. Show her the error in her ways. Show her that because she is alive that is your love. That because she is fed that is your love. Show her who you are. The great I am, my God! Hallelujah!" he yelled with real tears falling from his eyes.

Darby ignored his prayer and wondered what Qwote was doing. As Kirk stood up the nurse came in. She checked Darby's vitals and gave her some medicine. The doctor then came in and spoke with her about her injuries. She informed him that she needed to speak with the police, and he called them for her before exiting the room. Kirk eyed Darby suspiciously. He'd seen Darby do some sinful things. Daily he prayed for his and her salvation.

"Darby, what are you up to now? You're alive and well. God is giving you another shot at making it to Heaven. Why do you let him down like this?" he asked with sad eyes.

Darby smiled at what she had planned. She shrugged and felt the effects of the IV Motrin kick in.

"If there is a Heaven I've been canceled from making it in years ago, and you have too, nigga. You might as well find some more hoes to put on the stroll, so I don't have to pay your fucking bills," she snapped.

Kirk ignored her and sat down. Darby was now the one who took care of him, so he knew not to push her too far. What he did instead was pray for the people he knew she was about to wreak havoc on.

The minute Darby was released from the hospital she went to see her mother. She slowly walked into the worn down house that used to be so beautiful and she shook her head. Her mother was laying in her own vomit in the middle of the floor shaking. Darby was disgusted and amused by what she saw. Her mother was a living testament of what happened to the people that fucked her over.

"You look a fucking mess. No wonder my brother doesn't want anything to do with you," Darby said in a disgusted tone, and she went into her bag. Darby dropped fifteen dollars' worth of crack down at her mother, and her mother slowly grabbed it.

There wasn't much Diane could say. She needed the drugs and was two seconds away from selling her body to get them. Darby was all that she had so she endured the torment and disrespectful words in order for her to survive. Diane slowly stood up looking like something out of someone's worst nightmare and she walked away. Darby felt only a smidgen of remorse for her mother. She texted one of her younger clients that was always looking to please her and told him to come clean her mother's home and bring her some groceries.

"Aye, chick, don't use it all! I won't be back for at least a week. I met someone," Darby yelled.

Diana was too busy getting high to even respond to her daughter. Darby didn't mind she was in her own world as well. She started to blush as she thought about Qwote. She was falling more and more for him each day.

"Yes, ma, you heard me correctly. I've finally met a man that I love and can be happy with. Guess what, bitch? He loves me too! Damn, I can't wait to marry him!" Darby said excitedly and left out of the house.

Darby got into her car and drove to Qwote's building. What she loved the most was that Qwote was driven. Lourdes was only a social worker. Darby felt like Qwote should have been with someone who was on his level. Someone like herself who was self-made. Qwote was going places and well, Lourdes really wasn't in her opinion.

Darby watched people enter in and out of the building until she spotted Qwote walking out of the large brick building with his brother Quamir. They were both dressed dapper in expensive suits. Laughing and holding cell phones, they got into Qwote's midnight blue Mulsanne.

"Damn my man looking good," Darby said as Qwote and his brother pulled off.

Darby followed after them. She stayed back far enough for them to not notice her, and she watched them pull into a local pub's parking lot. Darby parked five cars away from them and watched them enter the pub. She freshened up her makeup and spritzed herself with some Bond.9 before exiting her car and entering the pub after them. She looked around and spotted Qwote and his brother at the bar. She smiled to herself as she approached them.

"Qwote, is that you?"

Qwote stopped talking to his brother, that was a year younger than him, and looked at Darby. She was dressed in skin tight, black jeans with six inch Pigalle pumps, and a black, fitted top that showed off her ample breasts. He made sure to not stare, but still took notice of how attractive she looked. He smiled at her as his brother openly stared.

"Damn who this?" Quamir asked.

Darby looked at Quamir. She'd dreamed of him some during her adolescent nights. He was always into Sundae so he never paid her any mind. She figured she would give his dick a ride as well when she got the chance; however, her main focus was getting Qwote. She wasn't sure why but she *had* to have him.

"Aye, Quamir, this Darby. She went to high school with us," Qwote told him.

Quamir scrunched up his handsome face as he tried to remember the bombshell that stood before him. The only Darby he remembered was… "Dirty Darby," he accidentally blurted out.

Darby's eyes grew wide and she quickly walked away. Qwote jumped up from his seat and caught up with her. He grabbed her hand, and she turned to him with watery eyes. Qwote felt bad at the moment for her. He grabbed her and pulled her into his arms. Darby was so excited to be near him that she made herself cry harder.

"Ma, it's cool, he didn't mean it. Fuck all that high school bullshit. Okay," Qwote said and she looked up at him.

"Okay," she said while sniffling.

Qwote nodded and led her back over to the bar. Quamir looked at Darby feeling like shit.

"Baby girl, a nigga didn't mean to say that bullshit. Can I buy you a drink?" he asked.

Darby managed a nod as she sat down. Quamir was fine as hell. He looked so much like Qwote that Darby knew for sure at that moment that she had to fuck him too.

"So, Darby, this is my brother Quamir. Quamir, this is *Darby*. She stays next door to me and Lourdes," Qwote said introducing the two.

They both smiled at each other and Quamir felt excitement move through him. Darby was fine as hell, and he was interested in taking her out.

"So, Miss Darby, would it be rude if I asked you out? Qwote got some tickets to a concert, and I was going to bring my friend, but I would love if you could accompany me," he flirted.

Another chance to be around my baby. Hell yeah, I'm going, Darby thought. "Sure I would like that, Quamir," she replied shyly.

Quamir nodded and looked at her breasts once again. He couldn't wait to slide his big dick between them. Darby had that Hollywood look to her. Quamir knew she would look fly hanging off of his arms. He was grown and past the young man games, but still he liked to have bragging rights, and Darby would give him a lot of shit to brag about.

"Cool then, it's next week. You'll get to meet the crew then," he said.

Qwote chuckled. "You one of us now, baby girl," he said and tossed his drink back.

Darby took in his cologne as she sat beside him. She could still feel his big arms wrapped around her body, and she was in pure bliss just from being in his presence. Qwote was that nigga.

"Yeah, I guess I am," she said quietly while staring at him and envisioning the future she knew they would have together.

Chapter Five

"How you feeling?"

Sundae slowly looked over at her husband, Drama. He was everything she thought she wanted, but what she felt she no longer needed. He'd gotten her pregnant the first time they had sex, and she later went on to have a miscarriage. The damage had already been done, however. Sundae had told Quamir she couldn't be with him, because she believed she was having a baby by Drama. She felt hurt, angry, and embarrassed once she lost her baby. She decided to stay with Drama and see where they could go. At the time, he was putting his all into making her happy. She had no idea of his flaws until it was too late. As time went on Sundae realized that Drama worked more than Quamir did.

Quamir was a lot like Qwote. He wanted it all. He worked all the fucking time. It was his only downfall. He was cheating on Sundae with his career, and she was lonely. She was in another state and whenever Qwote came to visit Lourdes, Quamir stayed home. He always found a reason to be busy. Sundae was tired of being in a long distance relationship with him. She wasn't like Lourdes. The phone calls and texts weren't enough for her. She decided to cheat and had been living with the regret ever since. Sundae appeared to have it all, but she was learning that the grass wasn't always greener on the other side. Drama was, in fact, cheating on her with his career as well.

She was starting to fall into a deep depression, because of her situation and just thinking of Quamir's sexy ass had her wanting her old thang back something serious. However, Sundae came from a family of high society. Her parents would cut her off if she was to leave Drama at the time when she'd first gotten pregnant. In their eyes, he was a good catch. Drama did make good money being a producer, but his money couldn't keep her warm at night. Often she fell asleep to thoughts of Quamir and the good old days. In the beginning, things were good with them until they weren't. Then instead of talking to him about it, she assumed he would just know what was wrong with her but he didn't. He started to pull back because she was always in a bad mood and she started to cheat. She ended up leaving him because she felt like Drama, whose real name was Draven, could make her happier and for awhile, he did.

Drama was cool. He was rich but humble. He loved the Lord, and he loved the hell out of her. It was only one problem. They lacked the chemistry that she shared with Quamir, and it was slowly driving her insane.

"I'm good, Drama," she said and rolled onto her side.

Drama climbed onto the bed and started to rub her back. He loved her too much to see what was right before his eyes. They were falling apart and neither wanted to acknowledge that fact.

"I don't trust old girl. I talked to my boy, and he claimed that the chick's name wasn't Darby, but I know that nigga. He was lying, Sundae. You don't need to be hanging with no bitch that's selling pussy," he said.

Sundae instantly grew an attitude. It didn't take much for her to get mad at Drama lately. They'd been back in Detroit for a year and had made a home there. Drama had even linked up with a lot of Detroit rappers and producers so he was good. Sundae had effectively avoided Quamir, but now with Lourdes being back, she was thrust into the same room with him. It was becoming harder and harder for her to fight the feelings that were still there. The fact of the matter was she was still in love with him. He seemed to know it as well, because he had her conceding to things that Drama wouldn't like.

"Why not? You're my husband not my damn daddy, Draven," she said looking for a reason to argue with him.

Drama sighed and sat back, he was not used to the angry side of Sundae. Lately, she had been snapping at him for no reason.

"Yeah, I am your husband so watch how the fuck you speak to me. Okay?"

Sundae wanted to talk more shit, but the tone of his voice told her not to. "Okay. Now, why are you tripping on Darby? She's cool peoples."

"Because I talked to my boy, and he lying for her. She was that chick in that photo. I don't need my wife hanging with some slut and that bitch look crazy," he stated.

Sundae turned to Drama. She looked at her sexy, mixed man and smiled. Drama was a lot of shit, but one thing he would never be was ugly. He was GQ model fine. What drove Sundae crazy was when he started talking in his New York slang. Her panties got so wet at that shit.

"Drama, how the fuck does she look crazy after just meeting her once?" she asked him laughing.

Drama licked his dark pink lips. He was a light skin tone that was pale in the winter and nicely tanned in the summer. "My abuela would always tell me that some shit you just pick up on people instantly, and that chick is crazy. I could see that shit in her eyes. Look don't ever invite her over here. I don't want that negative ass energy in our house," he said and kissed her lips.

Drama turned onto his side and Sundae thought about what he'd said for a moment before laying back down. She hadn't kicked it with Darby in years, so she wasn't about to have an argument with her husband over her. She would simply hang with her if she wanted to, and be sure to not invite her over to her home.

The next day Sundae sat nervously inside of the plush office. Was she wrong? Yes. Did that stop her from coming? No. She'd tried. She'd even prayed on it yet still she woke up and drove herself an hour away from her home, so that she could visit him. They hated each other most of the time, but there was still love there and well they weren't ready to let it go.

"What up? You feeling good?" Quamir asked stepping into his office.

Sundae swallowed the huge lump that was in her throat. Quamir looked so damn good to her. Standing at 6'2 with smooth brown skin, a handsome baby face, with low cut black hair that was waved up, he was everything to her. She still remembered falling for him in middle school back then life was so simple. So easy. Now she was stuck with decisions that were life changing.

"Yeah I'm okay. I brought your lunch. Um…we can't keep doing this," she said avoiding eye contact with him.

Quamir walked over to her and sat down. He grabbed his container and lifted the lid. He'd given Sundae up once, and he refused to do it again.

"What are we doing, Sundae? Is my dick in you? Am I making you cum, or are we sharing a lunch together as friends?" he asked and started eating his food.

Sundae stared at him. For the last month, Monday through Friday, she had been by Quamir's office and ate lunch with him faithfully. She knew it was wrong. She knew Drama would be crushed, but she also felt guilty. She felt bad for cheating on Quamir and leaving him for dead like she did. She told herself it was harmless. They hadn't even kissed, yet she felt like she was cheating on her husband whenever she was in his presence alone.

"I guess. I can't stay long."

Quamir glanced over at her with a frown on his handsome face. The only woman to ever give him problems was Sundae.

"Why? What the fuck you come for if you were bringing that stank ass attitude? I didn't do shit to you, Sundae. Save that shit for you husband," he told her.

Sundae rolled her eyes. She grabbed her car keys and attempted to stand when he grabbed her arm. Just his touch sent chills up her spine.

"Chill out. I missed you all weekend and you trying to leave me already?" he asked in a gentler tone. Sundae looked into his eyes. *Damn.* How could she leave him when she had been missing him like crazy all weekend as well?

"No. I missed you too," she quietly admitted.

Quamir smiled showing off his perfect set of white teeth, and he touched her cheek. "That's my girl," he said and went back to eating his food. "So tell me what's been up?" he said.

Sundae got comfortable on the couch and sighed. "Nothing really. I did two clients this morning before I came and I'm tired already. I swear I can't wait to have this baby, Quamir," she vented.

Quamir chuckled. "You'll be having it soon enough. You not gon' be too tired to make my special cake for my birthday are you?"

Sundae was a hairstylist but she could cook as well. Quamir missed her food and was anticipating getting his birthday cake made by her.

"You know I got you," Sundae said and locked eyes with him.

Quamir licked his lips as Sundae's cellphone started to ring. She grabbed it out of her bag, and her heart beat started to increase.

"Hey, baby," she said in a sweet tone answering the phone.

"What's up? You not at home. I need some of that, ma," Drama said a little irritated. He'd canceled on the shooting range with his boys, because he thought Sundae was home.

Sundae avoided eye contact with Quamir, who was breathing so hard he sounded like a damn dragon.

"Yeah I decided to go into work then I had to make a run. I can head back now," she suggested.

She could see Quamir get up and toss out his food. Also making as much noise as he could by doing the little task.

"Nah since you gone, I'll just head out. You better be home when I get back, beautiful. I love you," he said sincerely.

Sundae instantly felt like shit. "I love you too," she said and ended the call.

"So you only love him?"

Sundae looked up and Quamir was leaning against his black oak wood desk glaring at her. Even angry he looked sexy. In a black suit that seemed to fit his body perfectly, he was still very attractive to her. His strong jawbone, with his almond shaped eyes, and full lips made her wet. He had a muscular frame that wasn't too big, but just the right size. He often reminded her of the male model Willy Monfret from the Nicki Minaj video "Right Thru Me" only he didn't have green eyes, and his skin was much darker than his. Quamir was also decorated in tattoos that added to his handsome features. People often said he resembled Qwote, but Sundae didn't see it. She stood up and walked over to him. *Sundae, you playing with fire,* she thought scolding herself. She nodded because she knew that she was, however, she couldn't stop herself. Quamir sucked his teeth as she walked up on him. Everything from his scent down to the way he tilted his head drove her crazy.

"I love you too, yet you love this more than me," she said and pointed around his corner office that was overlooking the Detroit River.

Quamir smirked at her. "Is that right? Didn't know it was a crime to be a goal oriented motherfucka. What the fuck a chick really want from a nigga? If the nigga hustling, y'all want him to go straight. If the nigga ain't got no job, y'all want him to get one, then when you meet a man with a good job you complain he work too much." Quamir chuckled. He leaned towards Sundae until his nose was touching hers. "*You* don't even know what you want. I only ever wanted you now look at us. Our shit all fucked up now because of you. Why don't you go home to that hoe ass nigga of yours? I'll fuck with you later," he said and pecked her lips.

Sundae didn't wanna like the kiss but *damn* she did. It ignited something inside of her that made her body shudder and her panties get wet. Quamir ignored her look of yearning and went back to his desk. Sundae had no idea just how close he was to breaking the firm foundation that she stood on. She gathered her stuff and left without speaking another word to him. Regardless of what they had said, she knew that tomorrow she would be back on time with lunch for him.

Chapter Six

"Honey, how have you been? I can't even put into words how happy I am to have you home."

Lourdes closed her eyes and enjoyed the feeling of the deep tissue massage she was receiving. "Mom, I've been good. I'm so happy to be home."

"Who are you telling? We're glad to have you back. We missed you terribly, but you had to handle your business and that you did. We're so proud of you, babe,'" she said smiling.

"Thanks, Momma."

"So how is my Quinton," her mom asked.

"He's good. Still loving me how he should," Lourdes giggled.

Her mother, Carrington, laughed. "I know that's right! He better, my baby is special and only deserves the best. So when do you think the house will be done? I'm so ready for us to call Felipe," she said.

Felipe was Lourdes' mother's home designer. He was based out of Italy, but for his special clients, he always traveled.

"In at least a year, Mom. The crew is working fast, but it's still a lot that needs to be done. I do love the house…"

"But," Carrington said knowing her daughter. Lourdes sighed.

"It's just Sundae has it all, Mom. She has her own hair salon that's thriving, and I'm happy for her. She has her husband and now she's about to have her baby. Is it wrong for me to be envious of that?" she asked really wanting to know.

Carrington shook her head. She hated that she couldn't give Lourdes everything. If she could she definitely would have given her whatever her heart desired.

"No it isn't, but you also have to learn some patience, which is me and your father's fault. We've given you everything you ever wanted, so you don't have much patience when it comes to waiting but be still and let it happen. Quinton is a good man and he loves you. I can see it in his eyes, the way he stares, Lord it gives me the chills, Lourdes. Your father looks at me that way, and that's why after all of these years we're still together. Quinton will deliver on his promise to wed you. Hell if he doesn't I'ma kick his fine ass," she only half joked.

Lourdes laughed feeling an amount of pressure lift off of her shoulders.

The next day she walked through the mall with Darby. They were looking for concert outfits and having harmless girl chatter.

"Sooooo, who is this crew I've been hearing so much about?" Darby asked as they browsed through Windsor.

Lourdes picked up a cute, off the shoulder top and smiled. "It consists of Qwote, his brother Quamir and his two boys

Frenchie and Issa. You met them when we were younger or, at least, I know you met Issa," Lourdes said and smiled at Darby.

Darby looked at Lourdes and shrugged. "I did?"

Lourdes laughed. "Um yeah. Didn't you lose your virginity to Issa?"

Darby stopped browsing the clothes to think about the question. She honestly couldn't remember who Issa was. She thought back on her younger years, and she remembered losing her virginity to someone in Lourdes' basement, she just didn't know who it was. Back then Darby experimented with pills and Lourdes and Sundae knew nothing about it. She was often high around them. Darby covered her face and pretended to be embarrassed.

"Oh God yes," she squealed making Lourdes laugh. Lourdes hit her arm playfully and Darby rolled her eyes. *This bitch too fucking happy,* Darby thought looking at Lourdes. "Okay so Issa and Frenchie?" She asked getting back on the topic.

Lourdes nodded as she began to look back through the rack of clothes. "Frenchie and Issa are cousins. Now Frenchie lives in Atlanta so he won't be here, but Issa will maybe you two could become friends again."

Darby shrugged while smiling. "That would be cool. Oh and I fucked Quamir," she said nonchalantly and Lourdes laughed thinking she was playing.

Darby continued to look through the jeans until she noticed Lourdes was staring at her. She shrugged and gave her a gentle smile. "What? Men do it all of the time. He came over last night asking me out for drinks. We hit up a hookah lounge on Northwestern Highway and ended up fucking in his car. Shit a nigga in a $100,000 car deserves some pussy. Don't you think?" she asked and playfully slapped Lourdes on the ass.

Lourdes giggled but wasn't too sure about that. From what she knew, Darby had only known Quamir for a week outside of the past, even though she really didn't know him then. Darby picked up on Lourdes' judging eyes but ignored them.

This goody two shoes ass bitch. Bitch, yo nigga next, she thought and laughed. Lourdes smiled at her. "What are you laughing at, girl?"

Darby licked her lips while grabbing a pair of high waist pants. "Nothing just thinking about how much fun were about to have," she lied.

Lourdes nodded. "So how is your family doing, Darby?"

Darby's hand shook as she held the rack. She closed her eyes and counted down to ten. She opened them a few moments later feeling much better. "Um, they're good. My mom has completely done a turnaround. She calls me all of the time now. We're like best friends, but she has been sick lately, so I've been helping her get better," Darby said smiling at her own inside joke.

"What? That's so good. God is great, girl," Lourdes said.

Darby looked at her. *Is he? I wouldn't know,* Darby thought and wanted to say. Instead, she smiled and said. "Yep! He works miracles, girl."

Lourdes walked past Darby with a slight limp in her step. Darby noticed it almost immediately as she stared at her round ass wondering if it was real or not.

"You okay, girl? Did you fall or something?" Darby asked her as they went into separate dressing rooms.

"Oh yeah. Qwote wore me out the other night, then I had leg day this morning at the gym. So when I say my body is tired I'm not playing. I'm tired as hell," She replied.

Darby couldn't stop the scowl from sliding across her beautiful face.

"Oh yeah? Y'all be getting it in like that?" she asked slowly stripping out of her clothes.

Lourdes blushed as she thought back on how Qwote had licked her all over with whip cream then made her squirt all over his face. He was so romantic then nasty as hell at the same time. She loved it.

"Hell yeah, we do. Qwote can't get enough of this, and I can't get enough of him." Lourdes giggled. "Girl, I can still feel him inside of me," she whispered.

Darby bit down on her fist as she started to cry. She wanted to go into the other room and beat the shit out of Lourdes for bragging about fucking her man. *That stupid ass bitch! Oohhhhh! I can't wait to kill her ass!* She screamed in her head.

"Darby? You okay?" Lourdes asked.

Darby wiped her eyes as she pulled some coke out of her purse. She sat down on the bench and snorted two lines as quietly as she could, which made it sound like she was just sniffling.

"Yeah! I'm just so happy for you two. I always loved how good he was to you in high school. You're so lucky, Lourdes. So when is the wedding?" She asked and gagged.

"Um…soon I guess," Lourdes replied suddenly in a somber mood.

Darby noticed the mood change and she smiled. *Ha! Nigga must not wanna marry that ass! Ah ha bitch,* she thought.

"Well, I'm sure he will. When I saw him and Quamir at the bar he was talking about you so much. Plus, we're young. He and Quamir were both talking about kids being in their future when they hit like forty," Darby said and stifled her giggle.

"Forty? What…okay…well, let's just try this stuff on so we can go,'" Lourdes said instantly irritated.

Darby shrugged and started to try on her clothes. She could care less if Lourdes was mad, hell she hoped that she was.

Yeah, that's what yo ass get for bragging about my dick. Disrespectful ass hoe, Darby thought smiling to herself.

Chapter Seven

"What the fuck wrong with you?" Qwote asked looking over at Lourdes.

Darby smiled from the backseat as Quamir passed her an ecstasy pill. She took it and blew him a kiss.

"Nothing," Lourdes replied while staring out of the car window.

Qwote nodded while he bit down on his bottom lip. He wasn't in the mood for Lourdes' moody ass. He had a bad meeting earlier that day that resulted in him cursing out two of his VIP clients. He just wanted to chill with *Mi Amore* and here she was spazzing out on him for no reason.

"Look, I'm just checking on your ass," he said to her.

Lourdes rolled her eyes really not in the mood to even be around him. She still hadn't gotten over how he was discussing having kids with his brother at forty. What pissed her off the most was he was telling her thirty. It made her wonder if he was just telling her that to shut her up.

"And I said I'm good," she said back nastily.

Qwote chuckled. *Yeah okay. You gon' have this dick down your throat tonight for talking all this hot shit,* he thought glancing over at her. *And she looking good as fuck. Yeah, I'ma fuck her until she screaming for me to stop. Have that pussy talking to me,* he thought and chuckled.

Lourdes rolled her eyes at Qwote's chuckle. She knew him and could only imagine what he was thinking. They soon arrived at the Fox Theater and parked. Qwote's friends parked next to him. Everyone got out of the car and Lourdes was shocked, to say the least, when she saw Frenchie emerge from the white Evoque he was driving.

Frenchie greeted everyone then he looked at Lourdes. He smiled and they gave each other quick hugs. Lourdes walked back over to Qwote and grabbed his hand. He pulled her to his side loving and protectively. Mad or not they were a two for one deal. They always knew when to turn that arguing shit off.

"Darby, this my nigga Issa and his cousin my nigga Fred," Quamir said introducing them to Darby.

"Darby? Damn look at you." Issa said appreciating her new look. Darby smiled at him. He was looking good as well, but when she turned to Frenchie she had to do a double-take he was just that sexy. Frenchie chuckled while holding his hands up in the air. His wrist became exposed and Darby stared at his Breitling that was iced out. Yeah, Frenchie was fine as Quamir to her, but Qwote was still the MVP.

"Hold up, nigga, don't be saying niggas government's and shit. My name is Frenchie, baby girl. Nice to meet you," he said and grabbed Darby's hand.

Darby was hit with his intoxicating cologne as he kissed the back of her hand with his soft full lips. She blushed as she stared Frenchie up and down. Frenchie was hood, but so clean you couldn't say shit. You ignored his face tattoo and neck tattoo, because he dressed so fucking nice. His dreads were long, reaching the middle of his back. He had light brown skin with brown eyes and full lips. He was tall with a medium build to him and his swag spoke for itself. She saw him and instantly thought drug dealer. He was wearing labels from head to toe and shitting on all of the men except for Qwote, who was dressed simple yet looked so fucking good. Frenchie was wearing a turban around his dreads and even that shit looked cute on him. Darby discreetly winked at him, and he looked at her with his head cocked to the side.

Darby had no idea that Qwote and his boys were official. They didn't hate each other. They weren't secretly waiting on the next one to fail. They were, for the most part, loyal and because Darby was on Quamir's arm, Frenchie would never fuck with her. Even after Quamir tossed her to the side, like he knew he would, he would still pass on her. What Frenchie did do was make a mental note to let Quamir know he had a hoe on his hands, so that he didn't start catching feelings. Frenchie had let his emotions get the best of him one time, and he was vowing to never make that mistake again when it came to his friends.

"Aye let's go in," Qwote said and walked off.

"Good to see you back, Lourdes," Frenchie said to her.

Lourdes heart was damn near beating out of her chest as she walked alongside Qwote. "You too. How long are you visiting?" she asked.

"I'm not. A nigga decided to see what Detroit had to offer on the music tip. I'm working with that nigga Kasam on his rap group, and so I'ma kick it here until I decide to leave," he announced.

Lourdes felt like she could have just passed out. She was so nervous. Sweat beads were forming around her breasts and back. "Oh yeah? That's what's up," she said and snuggled up to Qwote's arm.

Qwote looked down at her as they stepped into the hall. "You off that bullshit, *Mi Amor*?" he asked.

Lourdes nodded looking up at him. "I am and I'm ready to have fun and see Futureeee," she sang and smiled even doing a little twerk that made Qwote glare at her before smiling.

Qwote then kissed her. All he ever wanted to do was make her happy. "Good because for all of that lip, you got some making up to do. Daddy just trying to make you happy," he said.

Lourdes' heart did a flutter at his words. Qwote was almost too good to be true. "I know and I love you dearly for that. You know how I get sometimes. I'ma Gemini," she joked.

Qwote chuckled. "Yeah your ass is two faced as hell," he poked with her and Lourdes bit his arm.

They messed with each other until they sat down in their seats. For the next two hours, they watched some of the hottest rappers perform. Future and Drake's Big Rings came on and Darby and Lourdes jumped up from their seats and started dancing. Qwote kept his eyes on Lourdes as she danced to the music. Frenchie sat down in Lourdes' seat and looked at Qwote.

"Man, who is this fine bitch that y'all got around us?" he asked and they both laughed.

Qwote rubbed his small beard while looking at Darby. "This chick Lourdes and I went to school with. She cool even though Quamir said she a bopper. He said he fucked her in his car and shit four days after knowing her. I gotta keep my eye on that shit, because Lourdes damn near love this girl."

"Oh, word? She knows her like that?"

Qwote nodded. "Yeah, Darby used to get picked on and shit and Lourdes and Sundae came to her rescue. You know *Mi Amor* got a heart of gold and shit," Qwote said getting caught up in the sway of Lourdes' hips. She was rocking some black jeans that looked painted on.

"Yeah I know," Frenchie said taking a peek at Lourdes. She looked better than she did the last time he'd seen her. He shook his head not wanting to disrespect his boy, and he went back to his seat. Jumpman came on and all of the men stood up. Qwote walked up behind Lourdes and wrapped his arms around her waist. He'd watched every nigga in the vicinity grill her, and he was amused by that because he knew that she would always be coming home to him.

He kissed her neck as she popped her ass on him as he sung the lyrics in her ear.

"Lobster and Celine for my Lourdes that I miss. Chicken, french fries for them hoes that wanna diss," he sang to her changing the lyrics somewhat to accommodate his baby. Lourdes blushed and popped her ass onto him harder. Which in turn made him hard as a rock.

"Stop that. My dick too hard, ma. You know I don't like that teasing bullshit," he said popping her kitty between her legs. The crowd was so thick no one could see what he was doing however Darby did. She was watching him like a hawk and unbeknownst to her, Frenchie was watching her like a hawk.

After the concert they ended up at the MGM Grand Casino hotel in a suite playing cards, listening to music, and smoking on some grade A weed. Lourdes had even taken two hits and since she didn't smoke she was extra high. She and Darby were laughing while they watched the men play cards. Lourdes was sitting on Qwote's lap and Darby was sitting on Quamir's lap.

"We should play strip poker," Darby suggested smiling. She was high off of coke and molly.

"What?" Frenchie asked staring at her with a deep frown. "Fuck we look like playing strip poker with two women and four dudes? Since Lourdes is Qwote's wifey that shit wouldn't be cool anyway. You reserve games like that for the hoes. Are you a hoe, Darby?" he asked with a straight face looking at her.

Darby laughed. She was too high to see Frenchie wasn't playing. Lourdes, however, didn't find anything funny.

"Frenchie, don't do that shit. She's dealt with that enough in her life. Leave her alone. She's fucked up, shit we all are, but that gives you no right to come at her like that," she said angrily. Quamir, Qwote, and Issa chuckled.

"Well the queen has spoken," Issa said and they all started back playing cards.

"Your girl Sundae ain't wanna come?" Quamir asked as Darby started to play with her fingers that were very interesting to her at the moment.

"Nah she was sick," Lourdes replied and Qwote shot his brother a stern look.

"Don't," he said and Quamir went back to his hand.

Sundae had cheated on Quamir in the worst way, and was now married to the man she cheated with and having a baby by him. Qwote felt like it was fuck Sundae, and he wasn't going to let his brother look like a sucker even asking about her cheating ass was not okay with Qwote. For the people he loved he could be very overprotective of them, and his brother was someone he wanted to see happy. Yeah, Sundae was beautiful but so were a million other women. He needed for his brother to accept that he had been played.

"Okay… so Darby let's go get you some water, you looked more fucked up than me," Lourdes said as she slowly stood up.

Darby shook her head and giggled. "I'm good," she said.

Qwote looked at Lourdes' ass. He dropped his hand and his boys all frowned. "Nigga, really?" Frenchie asked with his nose flaring. Qwote shrugged unapologetically.

"Aye duty calls," he said staring at Lourdes. "It's two rooms in this bitch, I'm gone," he said and pulled a giggling Lourdes off. Qwote took her to the biggest room and closed the door making sure to lock it. Lourdes immediately took off her clothes and Qwote took his off as well. He massaged his dick as Lourdes looked at him with a sexy ass smirk on her face.

"Come suck this dick, Lourdes," he said.

Lourdes moaned at the way he talked to her. She walked over to him and dropped down to her knees. She pulled his dick into her mouth with no hands as he stared down at her. He grabbed her head and made her look up at him.

"How much you love me?" he asked.

Lourdes let his dick go with a popping sound. "So fucking much, daddy," she replied.

Qwote licked his lips. He slapped his dick against her luscious lips.

"You better. I'ma love your ass until the day I die, Lourdes. I've only ever loved you, ma," he confessed and Lourdes started to go ham on his dick. "Shit," Qwote gritted out as his head fell back. He was experiencing pure euphoria. He started to pump in and out of Lourdes' mouth until he shot off down her throat. He picked her up and quickly tossed her onto the bed.

Lourdes climbed onto all fours and Qwote slid up behind her. He slid deep inside of her, and she moaned while clawing at the sheets.

"Mmmm, baaabbbyyy," she whined trying to scoot away.

Qwote slapped her ass while licking his lips. "Shut that shit up," he said and continued to slide in and out of her. Lourdes' head fell down and she started to throw it back at him.

"Do that shit. Work your dick," he encouraged and pounded harder until he felt her tighten her walls down onto him. Her body started to shake and soon he was blessed with all of her wetness. She was feeling too good to let up but rules were rules. Qwote pulled out of Lourdes and let go all over her round ass.

"Shiiitttt,"" he gritted as he came. He kissed the back of her shoulder and fell down beside her onto the bed. She looked at him as she tried to catch her breath and smiled. He chuckled as he tried to catch his as well. "I love you, girl," he declared before looking up at the ceiling and slowly allowing for sleep to take him away. As his eyes closed he could hear Lourdes say, "I love you too, baby, and that's something that will never change."

Chapter Eight

"So what are you wearing tonight?" Darby asked walking into Lourdes' bedroom.

Lourdes emerged from the bathroom looking like a super model. She wore a cream bandage dress that fit her curvy frame perfectly. Her short hair was cropped and cut to perfection and her makeup was on point as well. She felt beautiful and was excited about her girl's night out.

It had been weeks since the concert, and she and Darby were back hanging daily. Lourdes loved it, and Darby was happy that she got to see Qwote up close and personal instead of from a distance. Darby was still kicking it with Quamir, but that had run its course. She was ready to be with Qwote but until that happened, she would string along his little brother. Quamir was fine and his dick game was lethal, so she really didn't mind seeing him. His only problem was he wasn't Qwote.

"You look bad as hell," Darby said admiring Lourdes' beauty. *Bitch don't look better than me, but she cute in an average type of way,* she thought staring at her supposed friend.

"Thanks, so do you! We about to have some fun let's go," Lourdes said grabbing her clutch.

"What's all that shit in those boxes? I thought you finished unpacking," Darby said looking in the corner of Lourdes' room.

Lourdes looked at the boxes that were stacked high against the wall.

"I'm donating a lot of my stuff to this girls group home that I volunteer at on the weekends. They care about shit like UGGs and True Religion. I decided to give them all of that stuff, because I don't wear it anymore anyways," Lourdes replied.

Darby smiled but on the inside, she was boiling mad. *This bitch is always trying to show out. I swear I can't stand her ass. She ain't gon' do nothing but leave them how she left me,* Darby said to herself.

Lourdes started to walk out of the room and she stopped. She turned back around and looked at Darby. She knew that something was different about her friend, but until then she hadn't realized what it was. Darby had cut her hair just like Lourdes' hair. It was done so close to the style that it looked like they shared the same hair stylist. Lourdes liked it but was inwardly a little creeped out.

"Your hair, you changed it," Lourdes said touching her own hair.

Darby had forgotten all about the cut. She smiled while touching her neck. "Yeah I did some photo shoots for this man that wanted short hair. I didn't wanna cut my shit, but for fifteen thousand dollars a bitch said take it off," she said and laughed.

Lourdes laughed with her. "Fifteen thousand? Hell yeah, you did the right thing," she said agreeing with her.

Qwote stepped into the room and did a double take. He for one was so fucking tired of seeing Darby at their place. For the last few weeks, she had become a permanent fixture in their home. He knew he was going to have to talk with Lourdes about that then there was *this*. He couldn't believe the sight before him.

This bitch is on that Single White Female shit, he thought to himself and chuckled. If only Lourdes could really see all of the changes that he did. To Qwote, it looked as if Darby was trying to become his girl. He shook his head wondering if he'd smoke too much kush or was she really transforming into *Mi Amor* right before his eyes.

"What's up, Darby? I see you here again?" he said and walked over to Lourdes.

Where the hell else am I supposed to be nigga? Darby thought frowning at him. Although she didn't appreciate his tone, she loved his appearance. Qwote was on his hood shit decked out in dark jeans with embellished back pockets. He wore a black button up with a gold rope chain, a beautiful, black Hublot on his wrist, and black Timbs on his feet. He had on a black Detroit fitted, and he was looking so fucking good Lourdes and Darby were staring at him. He smelled like Kush mixed with some of his intoxicating cologne, and Lourdes couldn't wait to get back to him. Since she'd been home from college they had been fucking like rabbits. Neither one of them could get enough of each other.

"We're about to go, bae. Where are you sliding off too?" Lourdes asked.

Qwote walked by her and started to rub her ass. He licked his lips admiring her beauty. He gave no fucks about Darby being in there. To him, she was intruding on their time anyway. Lourdes glanced back at him and smiled.

"Qwote…we have company," she said slightly embarrassed.

Darby stared at them with watery eyes. They were too wrapped up in one another to notice. Qwote rubbed her ass again and then cuffed it.

"She in our room," he said with an attitude.

Darby walked away before he could see her tears fall and he smiled. Qwote pulled Lourdes into his arms and raised her dress over her ass. He squeezed her bottom before sliding his hands between her legs. He cupped her sex before sliding her thongs to the side.

"Qwote…baby, I have to go and the damn door is open," Lourdes said to him. Qwote looked up in time to see Darby quickly step away from the entrance. He frowned and quickly pulled Lourdes' dress down.

"You looking too good, ma," he said and kissed her.

Lourdes smiled at him. "Thank you; so where you going?"

"I'm about to hit up some spots up with my boys but aye…" Qwote walked over to their oversized bed and he sat down. He patted his lap and Lourdes walked over to him. She sat down and wrapped her arms around his neck. Qwote gave her a sensual kiss on the lips before speaking.

"Ma, why you got that damn girl over here all the damn time? You don't think daddy need some alone time with you?" he asked. Darby's blood pressure slowly rose as she listened in on the conversation. He'd already made her cry now he was talking down on her.

"But, Qwote, she doesn't really have anyone. Her mother is back being nice to her, but she said her brother refuses to even speak with her. She's always been shy, so she doesn't have many girlfriends," Lourdes explained.

Qwote looked at Lourdes and laughed. "Bae, that girl is far from shy. I'm starting to think she might wanna lick that pretty ass pussy you got between them legs of yours. Is that it? She been trying to sample my shit? She wanna eat my pussy?" he asked while slipping his hand between her legs.

Lourdes giggled while shaking her head and Qwote awarded her with a smile.

"She better not be. That's my sweet pussy, and the only one that can lick that shit is me," Qwote said and bit her playfully on the neck.

Darby was so upset she began to bit herself. She sunk her teeth into her wrist and squeezed so hard she knew it would leave an imprint of her teeth. She just wanted something to take her mind off of the pain. Her man was discussing eating another woman out, and it hurt her to the core. She was so wrapped up in her thoughts that she didn't notice Frenchie standing behind her.

"Fuck you doing?" he asked aggressively, scaring the shit out of her.

Darby let go of her wrist and jumped before spinning around. She ended up dropping her phone on the floor, and it got Lourdes and Qwote's attention making them emerge from the bedroom to see what was going on. They looked back and forth between Darby and Frenchie wondering what was the problem.

"What's wrong?" Lourdes asked adjusting her dress. Frenchie stepped up and Darby looked him in the eyes. She refused to let him tell on her.

"Frenchie was telling me about his case and why he actually left Atlanta. I guess he had sex with a minor and didn't know it, and now her people are pressing charges against him," Darby said.

Frenchie stood stunned at how Darby knew his personal business. He was beyond embarrassed that he had fucked a sixteen-year-old, hell he had met the girl in the club. She looked older than Lourdes with a body that was stacked like a motherfucka. He didn't even think to ask for ID. Now he was fighting the charges, but after dealing with such negative backlash he had chosen to just leave town. He looked at Darby and chuckled. He was ready to rip her head off of her plastic ass body.

Yeah, this bitch gon' see me, he thought.

"What? What the fuck is she talking about, Frenchie?" Qwote asked his boy hoping the shit wasn't true.

Frenchie scratched his beard. As he tried to explain to Qwote what was going on, Lourdes and Darby walked away. Lourdes was consumed with thoughts of Frenchie's case as they rode in Darby's new Audi to the club. Lourdes took the time to check out the luxurious mobile and she smiled.

"What did you say you did again? This car is nice as hell, girl," she complimented her.

"I work in sales. You got a nice car, Lourdes, and I should have one too. You not the only one with money and who can live good," she replied not able to hold in her disdain for Lourdes.

Lourdes pursed her lips and looked out of the window. She honestly didn't know how to respond to what Darby had said. Unbeknownst to Darby, Lourdes had so much money she was wealthy, only she didn't flaunt her money. She drove a cute but modest car, and lived her life as if she couldn't afford to hit up Gucci and Louis Vuitton on the regular, when in fact she could. Not only did her parents have a nice account set up for her, her grandparents did as well. Lourdes refused to waste their hard earned money on silly bullshit like $1000 shoes; she had nothing to prove. If she wanted to shop at Target she would. If she wanted to go to Neiman's she could. She'd witnessed Darby blow a few thousand on a shopping trip, and all she did was shake her head. Lourdes just simply wanted to know what kind of sales job Darby had where she could go to work whenever she wanted to, and have enough money to now own three luxury vehicles that all started at $100,000. She wasn't hating at all; she was just praying her friend didn't blow all of her money on foolish things.

Darby and Lourdes soon arrived at the club in downtown Detroit off of Congress and Shelby. They valeted Darby's car and paid more money to skip the line. They then went to the bar and had a few drinks. Darby could tell Lourdes was still feeling some kind of way about her comment, so she smiled at her.

"I was just bullshitting with you, girl. I really didn't know you were so sensitive," she said and laughed.

Lourdes looked at her. "Well, my mom told me that some people say how they really feel and often try to laugh it off as a joke. I felt like your comment about my money was out of line, but it's cool. Just know that I don't think I'm better than anybody, so if someone feels that way about me it's their own get up," she said and started back grooving to the music.

Darby side eyed Lourdes with a frown on her face. *Now the bitch thinks she's Oprah and shit. It's cool though, I got something special for your ass tonight,* Darby smiled while thinking to herself. After a few drinks, Lourdes and Darby were back to having fun. Darby had popped a molly and even slipped something special into Lourdes' champagne so that they could both enjoy the night, plus Darby didn't need Lourdes' complaints.

"Girl, it's hot as hell in here!" Lourdes yelled while fanning herself.

Darby nodded. That blow had her hot as well. She continued to dance until she spotted her friend, another escort, walk up. Darby smiled as she felt her plan coming together. She rushed over to the Brazilian and black beauty queen and hugged her tightly. Lourdes had never been jealous but to be around such beautiful, manufactured women had her looking down at her jiggly thighs, wondering just how good she looked in comparison to them.

"Palma, this is Lourdes. Lourdes, this is Palma. She works with me," Darby said, and she and Palma giggled at their own inside joke.

"Hi!" Lourdes shouted. For some reason, she just couldn't sit still. She had been dancing non-stop for the last thirty minutes.

Palma looked Lourdes over smiling. She only did tricks with women because she was a certified lesbian. Her head was so good they called her the Brazilian pussy monster. She couldn't wait to get between Lourdes' thighs. She ordered them all a round of drinks and poured some more liquid drugs into Lourdes' drink that would surely get her right. Palma and Darby sat back and waited for the drug to take effect, so that they could enjoy the night.

Lourdes woke up the next day with a splitting headache. She couldn't even open her eyes because her head was pounding so hard. She leaned over and hurled up everything that was in her stomach.

"Yes. Yes, I know. Well, I tried to get her to slow down, but she kept drinking. Look I know, Qwote. She was really fucked up, and I had to get a room. I couldn't drive back while intoxicated all the way out there, and she was passed out. Okay well, I'll text you the address," Lourdes could faintly hear Darby say.

Lourdes groaned and touched her head. She was in so much pain she wanted to cry.

"Qwote...baby," she whined while wiping vomit away from her mouth.

"He's not here yet, boo. You got so fucked up yesterday. Lourdes, I had no clue that you liked girls," Darby said while holding in her laugh.

Lourdes tried to look up at her but she couldn't. She groaned and closed her eyes.

"What? Darby, where is Qwote? I need him. I feel so sick," she complained.

Lourdes started dry heaving and Darby looked around the hotel room. Palma was asleep on the bed next to Lourdes and they were both naked. Darby started to check her phone for messages when she heard someone banging on the door. She smiled and jumped up. Darby always did blow so she never had a hangover unless she did too much. Last night was too good to miss, she had only snorted four lines which had her good and high.

"Where the fuck she at?" Qwote asked walking in the room with a pregnant Sundae.

Darby was shocked to say the least when she saw Sundae. What Darby didn't know was that Drama was out of town for the next few days, and Sundae had chosen to stay with Lourdes since they hadn't really hung out in the last few weeks. Sundae looked at the beautiful, messy hotel suite and shook her head. This was completely out of Lourdes' character.

"What the fuck was you all doing last night?" she asked taking in Darby's put together appearance.

This bitch looks like she just left out of the beauty salon, Sundae thought.

"What the fuck? Get your ass up!" Qwote yelled getting Sundae and Darby's attention.

Sundae and Darby rushed to the bedroom and Sundae's mouth fell open. She couldn't believe that Qwote was holding up her naked friend that was covered in vomit and in bed with another naked woman. The sight was so shocking she had to clutch her stomach.

"Oh my god. Lourdes!" she yelled.

Lourdes tried to lift herself up but the pain was just too much. Sundae looked at Darby angrily. "You couldn't have fucking cleaned her up? Bitch, you look fine to me so why my girl look like this?" she asked.

Darby looked at Sundae as if she was crazy. *Is this pregnant bitch talking to me? I will kill this hoe and that fucking baby,* she thought trying to rein her emotions in.

"Well she was asleep when I left out of the room," she lied.

Lourdes attempted to look at Darby as Qwote carried her across the room. He was so angry he could have beat the black off of Lourdes' ass.

"So this the type of shit you do when you go out? You fucking cheating on me, Lourdes?" he asked in an eerily calm voice.

"Qwote, can we please clean her up and take her home before you start going in on her?" Sundae asked thinking of her friend's health at the moment.

Qwote shot Sundae a look. "You probably encouraged her to do this shit seeing how you fucking cheated on my brother and shit," he said angrily disregarding Sundae's feelings.

Sundae's eyes watered. "Wow okay. Well, Lourdes is her own woman. I didn't make her get in the bed with that hoe. I didn't even know she was going out, nigga, so watch how the fuck you talk to me," Sundae said.

Qwote shook her comment off. "Yeah whatever," he said carrying Lourdes into the bathroom.

Qwote turned the shower on and then helped Lourdes step in. His eyes filled with anger as he looked at bit marks all over her breasts and shit. He shook his head while biting down onto his bottom lip so hard he almost broke the skin.

"Hurry the fuck up!" he yelled making Lourdes jump.

Lourdes started to cry. Qwote had never spoken to her in that manner before. She trembled as she washed herself up. She stepped out of the shower slowly, and he helped her dry off. After she was done Qwote helped her get dressed, and he grabbed her bag and phone. He looked at Darby, who stood by the wall with a blank expression on her face. Something about the whole situation didn't sit right with him. He was a man that trusted his instincts and something was telling him not to trust Darby. The bitch was just too sneaky for his liking.

"Aye, stay the fuck away from Lourdes. I don't wanna see your bony ass in my shit any fucking more, bitch," he said through gritted teeth, and him along with Sundae and Lourdes walked out of the room.

Darby heard the door slam and she slowly slid down the wall. She pulled her knees to her chest and started to cry. She couldn't believe her man had actually talked to her in such a way.

"He fronting on me for that pussy eating hoe? Wow. I can't believe him," she cried.

Darby shook her head as she thought about the mean things Qwote had spoken to her. She wasn't sure how, but she was going to do a few things. She was going to fuck Sundae up for talking to her in such a way. She was going to get Lourdes out of the picture for good, and last but not least, she was going to have her man. She could care less what

Qwote said. She wasn't going anywhere, and she would show him better than she could ever tell him just who the right woman for him was.

Chapter Nine

"When is the last time you've spoken to him?" Sundae asked.

Lourdes shoulders slumped as she stared at her best friend. She was in such a fucked up position. Not only had Qwote temporarily moved out of their condo, she had also had a surprise drug test at her job, and was suspended for having coke in her system. She was so mad she didn't know what to do. It was obvious she was drugged and what hurt the most was that it was Darby who had done it.

"It's been three weeks, Sundae. I called him yesterday at your baby shower, and he picked up only to tell me to leave him the fuck alone, and to stop hitting his fucking line. He keeps saying he need space, but I just can't do it. My heart hurts without him. I was the one that was violated, yet he's saying that I cheated on him. I just don't get it," Lourdes said and her eyes watered.

Sundae shook her head. She wasn't sure what to say. She felt so very bad for her best friend.

"I'm so sorry this has happened to you, boo. Qwote is a good man, but he wrong for this shit here. Where is that bitch ass hoe Darby at?"

Lourdes shrugged wishing she knew. "I went over to her place a few times and she never came to the door. Can you believe her or that girl actually posted a fucking video of me getting ate out on some porn site? My cousin called me and told me about the video. He loves porn and damn near pissed himself when he saw it. I reported it and got it taken down, but who knows how many more videos are out there," Lourdes said shaking her head.

"Wow," Sundae shook her head in disbelief. She looked up and almost fell from her seat. Heading their way was Darby and Lourdes' mother Carrington laughing and smiling like shit was all good. "This bitch is crazy," Sundae said getting Lourdes' attention.

Lourdes watched her mother walk up with the woman that had fucked her world up and she jumped up from her seat. She walked up to them and slapped the taste out of Darby' mouth. Darby stumbled and ended up falling down. Lourdes stood over her glowering.

"Bitch, you got a lot of fucking nerve! Stay the fuck away from me!" she shouted.

Carrington was beyond shocked by her daughter's behavior. She grabbed Lourdes and shook her arms. "Girl, what the hell is wrong with you? Show me some respect and sit your ass down," she said and let her go.

Darby slowly stood up feeling beyond embarrassed and extremely angry. Darby looked at Lourdes and started to cry. Lourdes wasn't fazed by her tears as she sat down and rolled her eyes. She felt a little betrayed by her mother.

"Mom, how could you be hanging with her? After all she did to me. Qwote left me, ma. My job has suspended me all because of her!" Lourdes yelled extremely hurt by her mother's actions.

Darby continued to cry while she did summersaults in her head. She was so very happy to hear that her man was away from his whore. She had gotten tired of sharing him with Lourdes. Darby hung her head not wanting to look Lourdes in the face, scared she might laugh.

Carrington took her seat and looked over at Darby. Darby looked a total wreck. She then looked at her daughter. Lourdes gave her a look that broke her heart. Carrington never wanted to hurt Lourdes, she was just trying to be the peacemaker.

"Baby, this girl came to me two weeks ago on her knees pleading for me to help her. She admits to bringing you around that nasty girl and accidently getting you drugged. You know I had your father look that girl up, and she has an extensive record. She's also been arrested for drugging someone else. I know Darby made a mistake but still she's very sorry. I've even called Qwote and told him about everything. He'll come around and you should too. At one point in time Darby was you and Sundae's best friend plus she's practically family," Carrington said.

"Family? How?" Sundae asked wishing she wasn't pregnant, so that she could beat the fuck out of Darby.

Darby cradled her flat stomach as she sat down. "Because I'm pregnant by Quamir that's how. Look, Lourdes, I can't sleep because all I do is think about you and what happened. My God, I'm so sorry. I prayed in church so hard that you would forgive me," Darby lied with pleading eyes as she stared at Lourdes.

"You're what!" Sundae and Lourdes both yelled with shocked expressions on their faces.

Darby slowly nodded. "I'm pregnant," she said shyly while trying her hardest to hold in her laugh. It was comical the looks Lourdes and Sundae were giving her. *Yeah, bitch, I'm not going anywhere until I want too,* Darby thought smugly.

Sundae snorted not believing a word she had said. She refused to believe it was true. Why would Quamir fuck Darby was all she could think? In high school, she had checked Quamir plenty of times for talking about Darby being unattractive or stinking. She found it hard to believe that even with her makeover he would give her the time of day. No, she just couldn't believe that.

"You a lying ass. When did you even meet Quamir?" Sundae asked making everyone look at her.

Carrington gave Sundae a look. "Watch your language around me, young lady, and Darby has been dating him for a while now she says."

Sundae snorted. "Yeah okay, since when? He didn't even like you in high school. When did you two become so close?' she badgered her.

Everyone looked at Sundae questioningly. Sundae shrugged. "What, it's a legit question. When did you two get close?" she asked again.

"Why does it matter to you?" Darby asked.

Sundae wanted to speak up but couldn't. She and Darby had a staring match until Sundae looked away. Darby gloated inside. *Yeah, hoe like I thought. You just mad your old thing wants this good pussy.* Darby bragged in her head. Darby gave Carrington a small smile and then looked at Lourdes.

"I'm for real, Lourdes. I really am sorry this happened to you. Can you find it in your heart to forgive me?" She asked feigning sincerity.

Lourdes immediately shook her head no which only further pissed Darby off. Darby thought of her father, the only man she would ever loved, and her tears started to release from her eyes. Carrington looked at her daughter who sat stone-faced alongside an angry looking Sundae then she looked at Darby. She couldn't believe her girls were behaving in such a way. She clucked her tongue in distaste at the situation that was before her.

"This is truly a mess, girls. Women are supposed to uplift one another. I can't get with this new age bullcrap. Girls being catty for no reason and things of that nature. Yes, when I was younger we had disagreements every now and then, but it was nothing this serious. When did women stop loving one another?" She asked hurt that her daughter was being so unforgiving to Darby.

Lourdes looked at her beautiful mother and sighed. "Please don't make me out to be the bad guy, Mom. I love everybody but this situation is different. I can't trust her, Ma. I'm shocked that you're even taking her side right now."

"I'm always on your side, Lourdes, so don't ever say that. I'm just trying to keep the peace. I won't be able to relax until I know that you all have gotten past this little rift. I signed you all up for paint classes and a spa package for next week. I expect you all to make it as well," she said giving the girls a stern look. Darby was the only one to give her a big smile. Darby wiped her eyes with the back of her hand.

"I promise to make this right, and I will definitely make it, Ma," she said.

"Ma," Sundae mouthed while looking at Lourdes. Lourdes shrugged wondering why her mother had suddenly grown so close to Darby.

"I'm not sure if I can. I might be looking for a job," Lourdes said and Carrington looked at her.

"Stop it. If that place lets you go then it's their loss. Now let's eat and go to the movies. I missed my girls, and we will welcome Darby back with open arms, ladies. Life is too short to be mad about silly things," she said.

"Silly things? I've lost my man and possibly my damn job. That doesn't sound like something silly to me," Lourdes said getting upset with her mother all over again.

Carrington looked at her daughter. They had always gotten along, and she didn't want that to change. "I know, baby, and

I promise things will work out. Let's please try to get through this meal," she pleaded and Lourdes nodded refusing to even look Darby's way. She literally had nothing to say to her.

Across town on the east side of Detroit, Qwote stood on his grandmother's old block with his friends talking shit and shooting dice. Qwote was most definitely a businessman, but what no one could do was take the hood out of him. He frequently visited the neighborhood he spent time in as a child and had invested a lot of money to rebuild it up too. Because of his company, the kids now had clean parks and even a center for them to play at. He loved his hood and the people in it. Around the holiday time, he threw free events to give back, and would always help them as long as he had it.

He was trying to get his mind off of Lourdes, so he was spending a lot of time at work and with his boys. He felt so betrayed by her that he didn't know what to do. His boys thought that he was tripping, but he gave no fucks that she had fucked a girl instead of a guy. In his eyes, she had still cheated on him. It hurt because out of all the years that they were together not once had he stepped out on her. In high school, he cheated frequently. He was young and thinking with the head between his legs, but once they graduated and he started to mature he kept his shit in his pants.

"So...I fucked up," Quamir said and blew smoke out of his mouth.

"What you do?" Issa asked him.

Quamir thought about Darby and shook his head. He was so sick about the shit she had told him a few days ago. "Man, I fucked up and got Darby's ass pregnant," he said and hit his blunt again.

All of the men looked at him as if he was crazy. They'd prided themselves on being successful, young, black men with no baby mommas. They all had a plan and Quamir was following a life plan similar to Qwote's, but one night of drinking, smoking, and popping molly's led to him fucking Darby raw and cumming deep inside of her all night long. He had never slipped up before, but with Darby she just did shit that turned him out. She was licking his ass and sucking his toes. He'd never been with a woman so beautiful yet so nasty. Hell, she said he could even piss on her if he wanted to. He declined but couldn't deny a woman as beautiful as her at your mercy was an ego booster.

"Run that by me again," Qwote said walking up on his little brother with his jaws clenched. Quamir took a step back and slumped his shoulders. He looked up to Qwote, he didn't wanna disappoint him but what was done was done.

"Darby's ten weeks pregnant. I fucked around one night and went in that shit raw. Now she talking about abortions are against her religion and shit."

"That bitch ain't got no religion," Frenchie said shaking his head.

"Who you telling? She has been on me so tough talking about we need to get a place together and shit like that. She must be out her fucking mind. Talking about she loves me. I told her ass to cook my favorite food, and she didn't even know what it was. I can't believe I got caught slipping like this."

"But how you know it's yours? This bitch obviously likes fucking," Qwote said looking at him.

Quamir shrugged. "Shit, I don't. I mean she looks stuck up as hell. She doesn't look like the type to fuck niggas raw and shit. All I know is that I did slip up and because of that I'll keep her around, but you best believe that baby is not leaving the hospital without taking a DNA test. Fuck that," he replied.

"Nah, I wouldn't trust shit she says," Qwote said glancing up and down the street. Qwote shook his head. Darby was becoming a real fucking problem for him. First the shit with Lourdes, and now she was pregnant by his brother. It seemed like she was forcing herself into their lives when she wasn't even wanted.

"Man, I'm telling y'all this hoe is crazy. The bitch pop up out of no fucking where and fucks all our shit up. She called me crying that bullshit about the girl they met at the club was the one that drugged Lourdes, but I don't know what to believe. Lourdes and this bitch were butt ass naked in a fucking bed. I swear I wanted to fight that Brazilian bitch like she was a nigga. I don't play when it comes to my shit," Qwote said frowning.

Frenchie looked at him and shook his head. He wanted to feel sympathy but he really didn't understand why Qwote was mad. Lourdes fucked a bad ass Brazilian girl. Frenchie didn't see shit wrong with that.

"I feel you but she was with a chick. I mean let her slide off that shit. It wasn't like she was getting dicked down my nigga. Now you can be pissed because she didn't ask you to join," he reasoned and smirked at him.

Qwote shook his head as he lit his blunt up. He was tired of hearing that shit. Cheating was cheating. He didn't give a damn how fine the girl was. If he didn't okay that shit with Lourdes than her ass was wrong. His boys could laugh all they wanted to, but he didn't give a fuck. He still felt betrayed.

"Look, I know in high school I was on one. A nigga was young, shit I was fucking all them young bitches, but we grown now. Since we been out of school, I have not fucked around on Lourdes, and I expect that same kind of loyalty from her. That shit she carrying between her legs belong to me. Ain't nobody supposed to be licking and fucking that but me," he said and put the blunt to his lips.

Issa, Quamir, and Frenchie laughed. They all knew how possessive Qwote could get over Lourdes. He had always been like that when it came to her.

"Man, you don't play when it comes to Lourdes ass," Issa said looking at Qwote.

Qwote shrugged as he thought about his baby. "Nah, I don't play when it come to her. That's why I haven't been home. I'm scared that if I go in there, I might slap her ass for even putting herself in that position. I love her too much to ever put my hands on her. This shit just got a nigga all fucked up. I can't stop seeing her sprawled out on the bed and shit looking like she done been fucked good and still looking drunk as hell. Then Darby's ass walking around looking like Miss America and shit. This bitch got on a full face of makeup and everything, but she couldn't clean the vomit up off of my baby. Had my girl out there looking like a fucking hoe. I wanted to hit that bitch. I'm telling you, Quamir, that hoe can't be trusted. I pray to God that kid ain't yours. You don't need to be tied down to no grimy bitch like that," he said.

Quamir nodded, he was praying as well. "I know and trust when I say I'm done with her ass," Quamir said lying. He wouldn't dare tell his peoples, but Darby was worth the risk in the bedroom. For some reason, he couldn't get enough of her. He didn't love her, hell, he didn't even care for her. What he did love, though, was how she swallowed his dick and still had room to take his balls into her mouth. He was well endowed. He didn't come across many women that could deep throat him without whining about the shit. Darby was down for whatever, whenever, and Quamir liked that.

Qwote studied his brother for a moment before speaking to him. "Yeah okay, nigga. Look, this your life. You the one that's gotta live with the bitch in it not me. Good pussy is just good pussy. You can find that shit anywhere. Don't let that hoe fool you," he warned him.

Quamir chuckled while smiling and he nodded. He'd heard the warning loud and clear and he was good. He had shit under control. "I'm good. No lie she can do some tricks with her mouth, but I'm not letting that have a nigga gone. I promise I'm good," he said and they went back to shooting dice.

Chapter Ten

Sundae busted into Quamir's office while he was talking to Frenchie. Frenchie looked Sundae over and chuckled. Sundae hated Frenchie, and he felt the same way about her. He was mad at how she played his boy, and Sundae was upset about the stunt he pulled in New York. She felt like he was dead ass wrong for what he had done, and if she didn't love her girl so much, she would have been put Frenchie on blast about that shit.

"Look what the cat drug in, though," Frenchie said while Quamir looked at Sundae.

Sundae rolled her eyes. "Fuck you and, Quamir, I need to speak with you alone," she insisted. Quamir licked his lips as he eyed her. Frenchie looked between the two and shook his head. He knew they were playing with fire.

"Quamir, don't get forgetful on me, nigga," he said trying to drop some jewels on him.

Sundae looked at Frenchie and smiled. It was everything but a friendly one. "Nigga, you wanna be funny? We going down memory lane?" she asked ready to tell his truths.

Frenchie grabbed his fitted off of Quamir's desk and his key fob. He refused to argue with Sundae over shit that had nothing to do with her. That was him and Lourdes' business. Secrets like that could ruin the friendship he had with Qwote and Quamir. He didn't take that kind of shit lightly. He put his hat on and licked his lips. Sundae was a beautiful woman, but she was nothing more than a stupid bitch in his eyes. Even when they were younger he had never liked her.

"It's all love, Sundae. Aye, nigga, I'm gone," he said and stood up before walking off.

Bitch ass nigga, Sundae thought watching him leave out of the office. Sundae turned her fiery gaze onto Quamir, and he held his hands up in surrender. He had been with her long enough to know her. He could see she was coming to argue with him.

"Before you come in her spitting that crazy shit at me remember whose baby you carrying, and who you sleeping next to at night. I'm not your man," he said and went to sit down at his desk.

Sundae didn't want them to, but her eyes watered. She started to cry as she tapped her leg on the floor trying to control the anger that was building up inside of her.

"You…. fucked that bitch? Did you fuck her, Quamir!" She yelled.

Quamir nodded nonchalantly and went to look at the papers on his desk. What was crazy was that he actually felt wrong although he didn't owe Sundae shit. That was just them, though. They held a connection that no one but them could understand. Their love was their own.

"I slipped up and now the hoe claiming it's mines," he admitted.

Sundae shook her head making her tears fall onto her cream blouse. Quamir hated to see her cry. She wasn't his wife, but she would always be his girl. He never wanted to be the reason she was in pain.

"Calm down. You pregnant, and you don't need to be getting worked up over this shit. I'm good."

Sundae looked at him and started to laugh. "Oh, you good? Shit, what about me? I'm married to a man that I feel like is just my friend while I watch the love of my life do him. Now he's expecting a baby with some hoe," she ranted and threw her hands up in the air.

Quamir sat back in his leather chair with his brows furrowing. "How the fuck you think I feel! You married that nigga, Sundae. You did that shit all because you scared to let your family and shit down. You chose them and that nigga over me. I'm sorry, baby girl, but I can't feel your pain. You put us in this fucked up ass position. This shit ain't sweet, Sundae. Yeah, we have lunch together but a nigga dick still gets hard, and I don't see you bending your big ass over the couch so I can slide up in it."

Sundae's eyes narrowed into slits as she looked at him. "Fuck you, Quamir."

Quamir chuckled. "That's what I been wanting you to do. Why are you playing like I didn't pop that cherry? You know you been dreaming about how this dick would feel up in you," he teased her while loosening his tie.

Sundae shook her head. Just because she'd cheated on him didn't mean she had to continue to be a cheater. She did have morals. She was trying to do right by Drama. It was just becoming harder and harder to do so.

"I can't," she whined wishing like hell she could.

Quamir nodded while stroking his beard. "I respect that but come here," he said.

Sundae walked over to him and stood between his long legs. Quamir sat up and rubbed her stomach gently. She might not have been carrying his baby, but he still wanted her to have a healthy child. He was always on her about her eating habits and things of that nature. He was also hurt, though. There was no way around it. She was living and married to the nigga she was cheating on him with. He felt bitterness and love towards her. It was a strange feeling to have at once.

"Stop being mad at me. You know you will always be my number one girl," he said looking up at her. Sundae blushed as she looked down at him. Quamir slid his hand around to her round ass and he squeezed it hard. "You came in here ready to bit a nigga's head off and shit," he laughed.

Sundae frowned. She was still very upset with the news that Darby could possibly be having his child. She knew it wasn't ideal, but she had always envisioned herself as the woman to carry his kids.

"I was and I'm still mad. I still love you," she said shrugging.

Quamir kissed her stomach. "I love you too, ma. I know we trying this friendship shit out, but you know I'm waiting for you. We both know who you wanna be with," he said staring up at her.

Sundae looked down at Quamir and lovingly touched his cheek. Of course, she wanted to be with him, but it wasn't that easy. She was married to Drama and having his baby. She was trying to put her family first.

"Quamir...I don't know," she admitted quietly.

Quamir nodded his head as he eased back in his seat. He was visibly hurt. He was tired of Sundae putting Drama's bitch ass before him. Sundae tried to lean towards him and he gently pushed her back.

"Backup, but you good. I get it. So what, I'ma see you tomorrow at noon?" he asked looking her in the eye.

Sundae stuck her middle finger up at him. She knew she was wrong but still she hated when he rejected her.

"Fuck you and yeah," she said exiting the office. She could hear Quamir chuckle as she closed his office door.

The next day Sundae sat inside of her stylist chair getting her hair curled. She'd been texting Quamir all morning and was wondering why he hadn't chosen to respond to her.

"Sundae, someone's here to see you," her assistant said walking Darby into the middle of the hair salon.

Sundae put her phone away and looked up. Darby looked beautiful as ever. She was starting to look like Lourdes' long lost sister, but aside from that she was still gorgeous in her black jeans with her white V-neck, and moto leather jacket. She smiled as she strutted over to a stone-faced Sundae.

"Hey. I came to take you to lunch," she said in a chipper tone.

Sundae looked at the time on her phone and realized that it was time for her to be picking up Quamir's lunch. She shook her head as her stylist sprayed her hair. Sundae usually rocked her natural curls. Since the weather was cooling off, she'd decided to flat iron her hair, and so far she was loving the new look on herself.

"Not today and I'm not messing with you like that, Darby," Sundae said getting up. Darby looked at Sundae as she started to wobble to her station to grab her bag.

"You getting that wobble that the pregnant girls get," she said and laughed, making a few of the other stylists laugh as well because they felt the same way.

Sundae ignored her and Darby took a few deep calming breaths. *Bitch, I'm trying to be nice to your pregnant ass. I can't wait to have Tevin fuck you up,* she thought following Sundae around as Sundae gathered her things.

"Okay, ladies I'm leaving out. I will be back in a few. If you all need anything just call me," Sundae said and walked out. Darby followed after her quietly until they reached Sundae's truck. Sundae unlocked it and turned to Darby. She appreciated what Darby was trying to do, but it was too little too late. Darby was pregnant by Quamir, or at least claiming to be. For that fact alone they could never be friends again. In Sundae's eyes that dick still belonged to her. She couldn't be hanging with someone that knew what it was like to be with her first love. Hell no, she wasn't that kind of girl.

"Look, Darby, I get what you're trying to do, and I commend you for that but I'm good. I mean you and Lourdes was always closer anyway, so go get back on her good side and leave me alone. I only need for people to burn me once and I'm done."

Darby looked at Sundae with a frown marring her beautiful face. "And what exactly did I do to you again, Sundae?" Darby asked confused by the hostility she was feeling coming off of Sundae.

Sundae tossed her bag into her truck. "You fucked with Lourdes so I took that shit personal," she said only telling half the truth.

Darby nodded. "Okay, I get it. I guess you were just looking for a reason to not like me. It's cool even though I've done nothing wrong to you. Well, I guess I'll go," Darby said dejectedly and walked off.

Sundae felt a little bad as she watched her walk off with her head down. She got into her truck and pulled off with Darby on her mind.

"Well, the bitch shouldn't have fucked Quamir. If she would have kept them leg of hers closed, we might have a chance to be cool again," she said heading across town to pick up his food.

Dominique Thomas

Sundae grabbed Quamir's corn beef sandwich, and went to another one of his offices, located in Sterling Heights, to meet up with him. She parked next to his newest car and took her time climbing out of her truck. Her stomach was really starting to cause issues for her. She was wobbling, always tired, and taking forever to do the littlest stuff. She didn't wanna think about it, but she knew that her little lunch dates with Quamir were coming to an end. At least until after she had her baby.

"Look at you leading the way with that belly," Quamir joked as he held the door open for her.

Sundae rolled her eyes while smiling at him. Quamir slapped her ass as he followed her into his office. He took his food, and they went over to his desk to sit down.

"So how is your day going so far, baby?" he asked opening his container.

Sundae sat down and exhaled. She was tired as shit. Her cell phone rang and she pulled it out of her bag. She looked at the screen and saw it was Darby calling. She showed Quamir and he shrugged and started eating his food. A few minutes later his cell phone went off, and he picked it up. It was Darby as well. He sent the call to voicemail.

"What the fuck is she calling both of us for?" he asked.

"I don't know. She was just up at my shop trying to get me to go out to eat with her. I wonder if that bitch followed me here." Sundae said getting a little nervous.

"Why the fuck would she do that, Sundae?"

106

"Hell, I don't know. Why would she be calling both of us at the same time?" she questioned him.

Quamir bit into his food while chuckling. "Ma, you so fucking paranoid. I'm sure it's just a coincidence," he said and went back to eating his sandwich.

Sundae's phone vibrated in her hand and she looked down at the screen.

Darby: Hey. I know you said you're done with me, but I feel like we're not over. You and Lourdes mean a lot to me, and I will do whatever I can to prove to you all that I care about y'all. Will you please meet up with me later? I love you like a sister Sundae....

Sundae groaned and put her phone away. "I swear it's like since she's been in our lives shit has been crazy. Now she's begging me to meet up with her even though I just told her I don't mess with her like that."

Quamir opened a bottle of water and drank half of it down. He then passed the bottle to Sundae and she drank the rest down.

"And why is that?"

Sundae shrugged. "Because of the foul shit, she did to Lourdes and because of you. If that's your baby, then I will never be her friend again."

Quamir shook his head. He got up from his seat and walked around the desk. He walked up on Sundae and touched her stomach.

"For somebody that's carrying another nigga's baby you sure is watching closely over the shit I'm doing. I'm pretty sure that's not my baby. Even if it is I'm not fucking with her like that, and you know it. You can do whatever you want with her, but don't cut her off on the strength of me. Shit she never had me to begin with."

"But are you still having sex with her though, Quamir?"

Quamir stepped back and licked his lips. Even after all of the bullshit he still loved Sundae, so he couldn't lie to her. He also didn't wanna hurt her. He touched her hair and slowly ran his fingers through it loving the new look on her.

"Worry about who Drama fucking, that's what you do, baby," he said putting the attention back onto her.

"Yeah. That means you are," Sundae said and pushed his hand away.

Quamir leaned towards her and kissed her cheek. He rubbed her stomach then found himself caressing her tender breast. Sundae closed her eyes as Quamir kissed her on the neck.

"We both know who I wanna be fucking," he said and sank his teeth into her neck. Sundae allowed for Quamir to play with her until she felt him unbuckling her jeans. She grabbed his hand and looked him in the eyes.

"No, Quamir," she said frowning.

He nodded and kissed her again. "I'm here when you ready," he said against her lips and went back to his seat. Sundae fixed her jeans.

"I'm getting bigger and well more tired. I'ma have to stop these meetings until after I have my baby."

"Cool," Quamir said not looking at her.

Sundae rolled her eyes. "Don't do that."

"Do what? You said you was tired and I understand. I'm saying cool. Calm your horny ass down. It's obvious your man ain't handling that shit right now, because you been grumpy as hell all fucking week."

Sundae glared at him until they both laughed. "I hate you," she laughed. "Now tell me about the birthday plans," she said getting comfortable in the seat.

Quamir loved to just be in her presence. He stared at her for a moment. Sundae still looked just as beautiful as she was the day he'd met her. Hell, she actually looked much better now because she had a body and had matured into her looks. Her wild hair was blown out and straightened with a spiral curl giving her a different but sexy look. Her exotic eyes were piercing into him while her heart-shaped lips, that were pouty as hell, were stretched into a smile. He wished that he could hate her. For what she had done he did for a moment, but the feeling never lasted. He knew that he wouldn't be right until he got her back and got revenge on Drama for taking what was his. He was working on getting both of those things done.

"Shit. I'm chilling like I always do. You know I'm low maintenance. I might go to Vegas for a weekend or Miami. I wish you could come, sexy," he replied.

Sundae's face saddened. "I know me too. Well before you go you should sneak away with me for a day. I wanna take you out to eat," she said.

Quamir licked his lips. "That's what's up. You already know that's the only gift a nigga really wants," he said. They finished the lunch date with talks of his upcoming birthday.

Chapter Eleven

"So what's up?" Kirk asked.

Darby tossed him his rent money. She'd tried some new blow and was a little fucked up. She laid back on her bed and started to rub on her nipples through her bra.

"I might need you to run up on someone for me, Kirk. This bitch named Sundae is pissing me off. She's one of the girls that was nice to me in high school but shit done changed. She's pregnant so don't hit her in the belly, but I do want you to slap that bitch a few good times and also rob her. I can't stand her ass," she said while looking up at the ceiling.

Kirk looked at Darby as if she'd lost her mind. His caper days were behind him. He was dealing with some serious shit. The only way he could even cope with it was for him to have God in his life. He was beyond hurting people.

"Pregnant? Darby, I'm not about to go fight this damn woman. I told you that I'm trying to be a better man. I can't do no shit like that. The Lord would surely frown upon that," he said and shook his head. He needed money but not that damn bad.

Darby shrugged. She was too high to even get mad at him. He noticed that she was in her own world, so he decided to grab his money and he left. Darby laid in her bed until she dosed off to sleep. She woke up a few hours later and went to check on her mother. She walked in the home she grew up in and found her mom sitting on the couch looking half decent. Diana looked up at her, and she blessed Darby with a real smile.

"Hi, Darby. Your brother visited me today. He said that if I can show that I wanna change, he will help me go to rehab," Diana said and scratched her arm.

Darby pulled some crack out of her purse and dropped it down onto the coffee table.

"Well I guess you won't be needing that then," she said and cocked her head to the side.

Diana snatched the small sack off of the table so fast that Darby laughed. She got the greatest pleasure watching her mother suffer. She hated her most of the time.

"So I'm having a baby, Mom."

Diana stared down at the drugs wishing she had enough strength to not take them. The temptation was just too great, however. When Diana wasn't high she always thought of her husband that died, and how sad she was without him. Her losing him was how she started to get high in the first place. Darby had convinced her to do some coke to take away the pain, and somehow that led to crack. Diana hated the way crack ruled her life, but when she got high…*Damn*. It was like just for a minute her life was good, like it used to be. Just for that moment, all was well in her life.

"Oh yeah. Who's the lucky guy, Darby?" she asked, not really caring.

Darby rubbed her stomach. A big smile spread across her face. Just the thought of having Qwote's child livened up her spirits. In her mind, she had replaced Quamir with Qwote and had even imagined the night that they conceived the child. It was one of the things she did at night to calm her spirits. Thoughts of Qwote always eased her mind.

"This fine ass man name Qwote. He's so sexy, Mom, and he has his own business. I mean he loves me so much, and I can't wait to have his child. Everything I ever wanted is happening to me," Darby said and blinked away her tears.

Diana fisted the drugs as her eyes watered as well. She was fighting a losing battle, because she knew deep down inside that she was going to get high. At least one more time before she quit. Darby saw her struggle and got up from her seat and sat down next to her. She placed her arm over her shoulder and hugged her tightly.

"It's okay, really. If this makes you feel better than do it. He doesn't understand you like I do. He only comes over here to judge you, Ma, so fuck him. He doesn't know your pain. I know you miss Papa because I do too. That's why I get high so that I can be closer to him. How about you go get dressed, and we can go buy you something from the store, then you can come back and get high while I cook you some food," Darby suggested.

Diana thought for a moment about what to do before conceding to Darby's suggestion. She stood up and slowly walked away with the drugs in her hand. Darby pulled out her cellphone and sent a text to her young boy that she coped blow from.

Darby: Hey I'm looking to give away a grand for anybody that's looking to make some money. I need somebody to be touched.

Tevin: Hit me with the stats and for a grand you know I'm down pretty girl.

Darby: LOL that's why I fuck with you. I might have to get some of that good dick when I drop off that money, but yeah I'll text you a time and a place later this week. It's actually a few things I need for you to do, but I'll holla at you.

Darby put her phone away and waited on her mother to come back. She'd lucked up when she found out she was pregnant and was kind of sure Quamir was the father, but only a DNA test would let them know for sure. However, until then she would use her little bundle of joy, that she planned on giving up for an adoption, to her advantage. As far as Quamir was concerned he was about to be a dad, so whether Lourdes liked it or not, she was still going to be around and didn't plan on going anywhere.

After Darby took her mother shopping they went back to her mom's home and cleaned up while talking about baby names. Diana knew that Darby was crazy but at the moment Darby was the only person that supported her, so she found a way to cope with Darby and pretended she was normal. Hell, Diana had bigger things to worry about anyways like her drug habit that had ruined her entire life. She only had Darby so until she was free of crack she would do whatever she could to keep Darby around.

Darby left her mother's home before night fall and went to Qwote's mother's home. She pulled into Aida's driveway and parked behind Qwote's silver LS600H, she smiled and rubbed her tummy.

"Baby daddy's here," she said as she reapplied her lip balm before exiting the car.

Darby's hair cut was fresh still looking the same as Lourdes, and she had recently gotten "Qwote" tattooed over her left breast in Chinese tattoo symbols that Quamir believed said "Quamir". Darby rubbed it because it was a little itchy as she walked up Aida's long walkway. Qwote and Quamir had given their widowed mother a beautiful home in Sherwood Forest that was just gorgeous. She had three floors of nothing but space. Her home was reminiscent of an old boutique style hotel that you would see in downtown Chicago or DC. Darby had first seen the home two weeks ago, and she was very impressed with it. She'd even stolen baby pictures of Qwote.

Darby knocked on the door as her heart beat increased at the expectation of seeing Qwote. She hadn't seen him since he'd picked Lourdes up from the hotel, and she missed him dearly. She was really falling in love with him and wasn't sure how much longer she would be able to stay away from him.

"Darby, hi," Aida said answering the door.

Darby smiled wide at her soon to be mother-in-law and she walked in her home. Aida was a beautiful older woman that was still in great shape with a peacefulness to her that many people lacked. She was a school teacher that loved kids, so she was excited to be expecting her first grandchild. Qwote and Quamir were her only kids, and she was eager to have a little person to spoil and love unconditionally.

"Ma, I'm so tired," Darby said while shaking her head.

Aida looked at her as she closed the door. She wasn't too keen on Darby calling her mother, considering this was her second time seeing her. She decided to address it with Quamir later since he was her son.

"I'm sure you are. Well get in here and let's feed my grandbaby. How was your day?"

"It was good," Darby replied stepping out of her six-inch heels. Darby followed Aida into the family room and Qwote, Quamir, and Issa looked up at her from watching TV. They all just seemed to stare while Darby looked at Qwote with longing eyes. He was looking good as hell in a Versace crew neck sweater with black jeans and Nike boots. She smiled at him then looked at Quamir who was eye raping her. The pregnancy was actually giving her a bigger ass. Darby was loving it. She walked over to him and gave him a passionate kiss on the lips making Aida clear her throat.

"Quamir, why don't you go make Darby a plate," she suggested.

Quamir pulled back and looked at his mom. He didn't wanna stand. Darby had his dick on rock hard. He sighed and discreetly adjusted himself before getting up. He grabbed

Darby's hand and pulled her into the kitchen. He patted her ass before walking over to the stove.

"What you do today, Darby, outside of breaking into my Facebook page?" he asked turning his back on her.

Darby cracked a smile. She'd been in Qwote's Facebook account numerous times but for some reason he'd decided to change his password. She could no longer hack into it, so she had no choice but to hack Quamir's page. She didn't see anything but messages from thirsty ass girls trying to hook up with him.

"I don't know what you're talking about, baby," she said with a straight face.

"Quamir." He looked back at her. "My name is Quamir, and I know you were in my shit. I got an alert that said you logged in from your iPhone at noon. Don't fucking play with me. Stay out of my shit, Darby," he snapped and went back to making her plate.

Darby smiled. She loved when Quamir pulled his tough tone attitude with her. That type of shit turned her on. She popped her neck as she took in Quamir's good looks. Quamir was no Qwote but damn he was fine as hell too, and so easy on the eyes. He stood before her in black sweats looking like he had just walked off of somebody's gym floor. What Darby loved most about Quamir was his eyes. They were slanted and always dropped low like he was high, but they gave him this sexy bedroom look that she couldn't get enough of. Plus, he had a big dick. What girl wouldn't love that? He was so handsome he was bordering on pretty, but he had this thuggish demeanor to him that made him irresistible. She could see why Sundae was so wrapped up on him when they were younger.

"I'm sorry for going through your stuff, Quamir, but I took my mother shopping and dropped off some medicine to her."

Quamir nodded. "Don't do that shit again, Darby. I don't fucking play around like that. We grown out here and you doing that high school bullshit. Now, did you tell her about your baby?"

Darby rolled her eyes. Quamir had been calling it her baby since the moment she had told him. "Quamir, please don't start that shit. You know this is your baby too," she said.

Quamir chuckled. "I don't know shit until the DNA test come back. I'm still hot with you over all this slick shit you doing, Darby. Nobody told you to bring your ass over here and meet my fucking mother. You gon' make me hurt your ass," he warned her

Darby giggled. She waved her hand in the air dismissing Quamir. "Well I did, and it's done so stop crying over spilled milk, nigga," she said laughed.

Quamir brought Darby her plate and grabbed her by her neck. He made sure to look her in the eyes as he stared down at her.

"Bitch, don't think because it's a possibility that kid is mines that you gon' talk me to however you want. You better listen to me when I tell you shit, Darby, before I fuck you up. Are we clear on that?" he asked.

Darby nodded while staring up into his eyes. Damn she loved a man that took charge. Quamir let her neck go, and she started to massage his dick through his jeans. He slapped her hand away and she grabbed his dick again. She slid her hands in his pants and licked her lips as Qwote stepped into the kitchen. Quamir tried to pull back but he couldn't. Darby had a vice grip on his shit and was jerking the hell out of his dick.

"Aye, we about to go have a drink. You coming?" Qwote said to Quamir's back that was tense as hell.

Darby jerked just the head of Quamir's dick, because she knew he loved that shit. He swallowed hard. He'd never before met a bitch that he wanted to kill and kiss at the same time.

"Yeah... damn... give me a minute," Quamir said with a shortness of breath.

Darby tried to look around him at Qwote, but he grabbed her face. She smirked up at him and Qwote shook his head.

"Yeah okay. Don't forget what I said nigga and we'll be outside," Qwote said and walked away.

Quamir leaned down and bit into Darby's neck as he came in her hand. Was she a bitch? Yeah. Was she doing some crazy shit to him? Yeah, but the dog in him loved it. He couldn't explain why. He only knew that you had to experience the shit to understand it.

"Aye don't do no shit like that again. Something is wrong with your ass," he said as she pulled her hand out of his pants and licked the cum off her fingers.

Darby smiled. "Well if something is wrong with me then something is definitely wrong with you. I wanted to talk to you about your birthday. I was thinking we could go up to this cabin I own up north and celebrate."

"On what day?" Quamir asked thinking of Sundae and his date with her.

Darby watched him walk around the kitchen with an attitude. "Why the fuck does the day matter?"

Quamir smiled at her showing off his dimples. "Calm your ass down for one. You gon' make me choke the shit out of you, Darby. I'm not gon' keep repeating this shit, sweetheart. The day matters because I fucking said it does, now which day and I pray you answer me the right way," he said giving her a stern look.

Darby calmed down a little. She knew she was crazy but something was telling her that Quamir was a little crazy too, so she didn't wanna push it.

"I was thinking we could all head out that Friday before," she replied calmly.

Quamir walked over to her and caressed her cheek. "See that wasn't so hard. Friday is cool. We'll talk some more during the week, and I'll see who all wants to go. I'm about to head out so I'll holler at you," he said and patted her shoulder before walking out of the kitchen.

Darby rolled her eyes extremely irritated with him and finished eating her food. She was throwing the party to be able to be closer to Qwote. She really gave no fucks as to what Quamir was doing for his birthday.

"Shit the nigga could die for all I care," she mumbled and started to laugh.

The next day Darby sat inside of the courthouse with her lawyer. They talked leisurely while waiting on the judge to walk in. Every now and then Darby would glance over at the defendant and give him a warm smile. She was feeling sick from morning sickness but didn't let it deter her from dressing like she was headed for the runway. She wore a black, two-piece, tailored suit with a soft pink collared shirt and black stilettos. Her hair was curled perfectly in short curls, and she wore light makeup that gave her a look that screamed attractive but not slutty.

The judge soon walked in and everyone stood up. After he was seated they all sat down, and he began to go over the case regarding her assault at the hotel room. He looked at the defendant and shook his head.

"She had a restraining order out on you. I specifically told you that if I was to see you back in here you would be going to jail. As a school principal I would expect so much more from you," he lectured to the handsome, older, white man.

The defendant's lawyer stood up. "Your honor. My client was not the person who did this to the plaintiff," he spoke up.

The judge looked at him. "Okay well, where was he?"

The lawyer looked at his client. Darby smiled on the inside. *He can't say because his ass was in that same hotel cheating on his new fucking wife,* she thought while sitting with a sullen look on her beautiful face.

"He was away on business, your honor."

The judge snorted. "I'm sure he was. We've been given papers with his name checked into a room there. I'm going to sentence him to ninety days in jail for this. If I see him again, I won't go so easy on him," he said and banged his gavel.

The principal dropped his head and sighed. Darby had been wreaking havoc on his life for the last three years. He had moved twice because of her and still she found him with more false accusations. Her lies were so intricate that the police instantly believed her. It also didn't help that she was attractive with money. They felt that someone who looked the way she did didn't need to lie on an older, middle aged, white man. He'd lost his first wife and his job, because of Darby's lies. He was now about to lose another job because of her. He didn't even know what he had done to make her hate him.

"We got that bastard," Darby's lawyer said smiling.

Darby smiled as she stood up. She locked eyes with her ex-high school principal that was being obtained, and she smiled ruefully at him. *Hmm, I bet he wishes someone would just help him,* she thought and then walked out of the courtroom with her lawyer. They said goodbye and Darby headed off to meet up with a new client. Baby on the way or not, money was always on her mind. She wasn't going to let something like a developing fetus stop her from getting it.

Chapter Twelve

Lourdes: I miss you

Qwote: IMY too

Lourdes: Then why aren't you home? It's been two months Qwote! I was the one that was violated.

Qwote: I'll fall through after I leave this bar

Lourdes: K

Lourdes sat her phone down onto the bed and rushed to get cleaned up. She'd been a little lazy since Qwote had been gone. She hadn't wanted to do anything. She was starting to look for a new job just in case her current one didn't call her to come back, and she missed her man terribly.

Lourdes cleaned her condo in rapid time then took a long hot bath while blasting Eric Beringer. She sipped on her wine and prayed that Qwote would come home, fuck her good, and then move back in. She understood that he was mad, but he was really treating her as if she agreed to it. She was drugged and raped. In her eyes, she felt like she was the one that should have been mad.

"Oh he gon' give me some of that good dick tonight," Lourdes said and finished her drink.

Once Lourdes was done with her bath, she got out and applied honey scented oil all over her body. She slipped on a lace teddy with the breasts and vagina cut out and made herself another drink. She sat on her bed and let Eric's melodic voice take her away as he sung about making it up. She nodded her head while she listened to the music.

'Put on that song that you like. Girl, this that song that you like. Put on that song that you like. I know this that shit that you like. So let me make up for it.'

"Am I the one making up for it, or is it you?" Qwote asked looking down at her.

Just the sound of his deep baritone voice made her pussy wet. Lourdes closed her eyes trying to rein in her emotions. It was a very hard thing to do. She'd missed her man.

"You. You know I would never willingly hurt you," she said with her eyes still closed.

Qwote eyed her sexy body as his dick swelled up in appreciation at the sight before him. He licked his lips and pulled off his t-shirt only leaving him standing in his beater with his jeans sagging low and his black diamond Jesus piece chain. He held a styrofoam cup in his hand with a small smile on his face. As mad as he still was, he couldn't even front any longer. He missed the fuck out of his baby, and he was about to show her just how much.

"Look at me," he demanded and fondled her breast.

Lourdes gasped. "Quinton," she moaned calling him by his real name.

Qwote bent down and pulled her hard nipple into his mouth. He used the ice from his drink too slowly swirl it around her areola. Lourdes moaned and rubbed her thighs together.

Qwote put his cup onto the nightstand and used his free hand to slide it down between her legs. He slowly rubbed her vagina and groaned. She was wet like he knew she would be. He started to kiss around her breast before moving up to her lips. As his lips captured hers Lourdes opened her eyes. She stared back at him as she started to cry. Qwote stuck two fingers inside of her while gently sucking on her tongue.

The love was still there. No amount of time could take that away from them. He pulled back from her lips and stared at her. He gave her a sexy smiled that made her wetter and warmed her heart before he started to kiss on her neck.

"I'm sorry that bullshit happened to you, ma. I should have been there for you instead of leaving but I was upset. It's no excuse but it's the truth. I fucked up so let me make it right," he whispered before pulling her to the edge of the bed and spreading her legs open.

Qwote looked over her pussy that he felt was more his than it was hers, and he licked his lips. Just the thought of someone else sampling his shit had him wanting to commit murder. He wasn't a killer and never claimed to be, but for his baby, he would do whatever.

"If I ever see that bitch again it's over for her ass," he said referring to Palma. Palma had skipped town, and now had a bench warrant out for her arrest for drugging Lourdes.

Lourdes went to reply and Qwote caught her clitoris between his lips. He tugged on it until it swelled and he bit it. Lourdes moaned and grabbed the sheets. She tried to close her legs and Qwote shot her a look.

"Ma, I haven't tasted my pussy in months. You better open these fucking legs," he said and went back to sucking on her.

Lourdes bit down onto her bottom lip and stared at him. Qwote had been smoking all day long because he'd been missing his *amor* then Frenchie had stopped by with some lean, so he was definitely on one. He'd sipped just enough to have him the right kind of fucked up. He had some big business meetings coming up, so he would have to be drug-free for at least a month, he'd over done it with the kush but he didn't regret it.

"Mmmm she tastes so good too. I missed you," he said in-between his licks. He straightened his tongue and started sticking it in and out of Lourdes. "My pussy," he stuck it back in and slowly swirled it around before pulling it back out. "Taste so fucking," He stuck it back in and vibrated it inside of her making her legs shake before pulling it out. "Sweet," he said and started back sucking on her clitoris.

"Qwote...baby...I can't," Lourdes moaned with a jittery feeling in her stomach. She could feel some shit brewing inside of her that she had never felt before. "It feels...Qwote...Shiiitttttttt," she moaned and started to stream all over his tongue. Qwote sat back and watched her let loose. His dick grew so hard it began to hurt.

"That's what the fuck I'm talking about," he grinned.

Qwote waited for Lourdes to stop before he took off his clothes and climbed onto the bed. He went to the front of the bed and sat down. Lourdes tried to climb on his lap and he shook his head.

"Nah, turn around," he told her.

Lourdes nodding still reeling from her powerful climax and reversed cowgirl on Qwote while he sat up in the bed. They both moaned as she slowly pushed herself down onto him. He slapped her ass and she whimpered.

"Ride it," he said and licked his lips.

Lourdes rocked herself back and forth as she slowly went up and down onto his dick while being on her knees. The position that they were in was so hard for Lourdes because she could feel all of what Qwote had to offer. After a few months of no sex, she wasn't taking it how she did before. Hell, she had just gotten used to getting it on the regular before he left.

Lourdes tried to only ride the tip and Qwote slapped her ass. He yanked some of her hair up and shoved all of his dick inside of her.

"*Mi Amor*, you better stop playing with a nigga and ride your dick," he said before letting her hair go.

Lourdes closed her eyes and made all sorts of fuck faces as she rode Qwote into oblivion. She mustered up the strength to take the pain, because what type of woman would she be if she couldn't take her man's dick? She refused to allow that. Shortly after, he was cumming all over her ass, and she was falling onto the bed so spent that she couldn't even move. Her pussy was most definitely swollen. Qwote grabbed her a wash cloth and held it against her for a while until she started to snore, then he took it away and slid back into the bed behind her. He wrapped his arms around her body and held her as he got lost in his own thoughts. His jealous, stubborn side was telling him to leave but he couldn't. The same way he loved Lourdes to death, she loved him to death as well, and her love had put a hold on him that night. It was so strong it refused to let him get his black ass up and walk up out of that condo, He simply closed his eyes and went to sleep feeling better than he had in months.

The next day Qwote and Lourdes went to check on the progression of their new home that was being built. Qwote pulled onto the lot and he and Lourdes could see the actual foundation. They both smiled as they exited the car. The Michigan weather was cooling off so they both wore lightweight, leather jackets to deal with the weather.

"Oh my God, baby, look at our house," Lourdes said excitedly.

Qwote looked over at her. Just being in her presence had him feeling whole. There was no doubt about it she was the piece that completed him. She was put on earth just for him. He refused to ever again let someone fuck up what they had, and what they were building. He pulled Lourdes into his arms and looked down at her. She was cheesing so hard it made him chuckle.

"Ma, I'm so fucking happy to be with you again. A nigga was going into work mad then a motherfucka," he said and they both laughed.

Lourdes leaned up and kissed him gently on the lips. "I've missed you too. I especially missed seeing you in these sexy ass suits," she said and giggled.

Qwote was back on his business tip. Dressed in a black tailor-made suit with his Prada's on, and Lourdes just loved how her man could rock any look, and looked good as hell doing it.

"Shit, daddy gotta get to the money so I can keep up with you. I know your bank account looking nice you just never say it," he said and let her go.

Lourdes just smiled at his reply. What she didn't like to discuss was her money. Not even with Qwote, because she never wanted him to be intimidated by it, so the best way to avoid that was to not talk about it. Qwote didn't know how much she had and it was better that way.

"Whatever; let's go check on this house," she said grabbing his hand.

For the next thirty minutes, they walked through their home that would soon have four bedrooms and three bathrooms with an Olympic size pool and basketball court for

Qwote and his boys. As they left, after talking with the contractor, Lourdes was on cloud nine until Qwote spoke.

"So yeah Quamir's birthday party is next week, and Darby's throwing him a celebration at her cabin up north. I flat out told the bitch no, but moms been on my head about being nice to her, because she's pregnant and shit so I said I would go. No matter what you do, *Mi Amor,* don't trust that bitch. Okay?" he asked looking over at her as they sat inside of his car.

Lourdes nodded. She looked at Qwote and sighed. She was so fucking tired of Darby being in their lives. She was like that one roach that you wanted to catch to kill, but you couldn't because it was fast as hell. Darby seemed to always be one step ahead of them. She went from being a thing of the past to a permanent fixture in their lives.

"It's just so weird because she even hangs with my mom now, Qwote. She calls her ma and shit like she's been keeping in contact with her all these years when I know she hasn't. She has my mom checking me like I was the one in the wrong. Sadly, my relationship with my mom has suffered because of it," Lourdes said with a pout.

Qwote rubbed her thigh. "Aye don't let nobody pull you away from your moms. You love her, and I know for a fact she loves you. Your mother is a lot like you, baby. She sees the good in everybody. That's where you get that shit from, so don't be angry with her. She's not used to dealing with snake ass motherfuckas like Darby," Qwote said.

Lourdes nodded feeling a little better. It felt good to have her man tell her everything would be okay. He had always been a good listener.

"I know she's just so comfortable with my mom, Qwote. This shit is really pissing me off," she said angrily.

Qwote chuckled amused that Darby was playing both of their moms.

"That's the same thing that crazy hoe doing to me. The bitch is after something. You know Quamir got some settlement money from getting sick at that restaurant when we were younger. My mom, being overly cautious of our future, put it in some cd's for him, and the shit is a nice ass amount now. I hope and pray he don't tell that bitch about that shit. It's just hard to talk to him now, because she got him so fucking whipped, and he don't even know it. I mean she done did some fucking voodoo on my damn brother," Qwote said and they both laughed.

"Well, whatever she's doing I want no parts of it. My job still won't let me come back, and I almost lost you because I was hanging out with her. You know me, Qwote, I don't like drugs."

Qwote shook his head. "Nah, but I know something you do like," he said and grabbed his dick.

Lourdes blushed and shook her head. With men, any conversation could always go back to sex.

"I'm so sore it's not even funny. I'ma have to take my ass home, so I can soak her in the tub. All you can do for me when you get home today is cook me some food and rub my back," she said and laughed.

Qwote started his car up and pulled off. "Yeah okay. I'll do all of that and what you gon' be doing for me is sucking this dick," he said and chuckled before Lourdes punched him in the arm.

Chapter Thirteen

"This is dope," Quamir said looking around the Italian restaurant that was closed down for the evening just for them.

Sundae smiled. She had been fucking Drama all morning, because he was headed to the Chi for a few days. She was extremely tired, but she refused to miss a date with Quamir. She had even put on a black dress and done up her makeup. She knew the owner of the restaurant and asked them to close it down for her as a gift. Being as though she was somebody special to them, they happily obliged.

"I'm happy you like it. I've been having contractions," she confessed.

Quamir sat up in his seat and looked at her worriedly. He was on his fly shit and dressed up his dark jeans with a white collared shirt, and a black, Tom Ford suit jacket with some Bally sneakers. Sundae looked amazing to him in her dress and smoky eye makeup, but hearing talks of her contracting had him worried.

"Oh yeah? Did you tell Drama?"

Sundae nodded. She loved to see him so concerned. She wasn't even carrying his child yet he cared. Shit if that wasn't love she didn't know what was.

"They're just Braxton hicks' contractions, baby," she said and smiled at the term of endearment that easily slipped from her lips. Quamir smiled at it too.

"Baby? So I'm baby now or am I daddy?" he asked.

Sundae blushed. "Quamir cut it out. I'm happy I was able to see you. I've been looking forward to this," she said.

Quamir's cell phone started to ring the same time as the waiter walked up. As Sundae gave them her order Quamir turned his cell phone off. He then gave the waiter his order and Sundae looked over at him with narrowed eyes.

"Ma, we not about to do this. Do you be on your baby daddy like this?" he asked with an amused look on his handsome face.

Sundae shook her head. "I don't have to be on him like that, because he doesn't have bitches calling his phone."

Quamir laughed. "That you know of," he said and she sat up in her seat. He laughed harder while shaking his head. "I'm just fucking with you so calm your ass down. Now what did you get me?" he asked.

Sundae looked at him angrily for a moment before deciding to let it go. Their time together was already limited. She didn't wanna ruin it by arguing with him. Sundae grabbed her purse from the nearby chair that she had sat it in, and she pulled out a small watch box. She handed it to Quamir, and he smiled so wide it made her heart beat a little bit faster.

Quamir looked at the green box that held the gold crown on the edge of it. He opened it and was impressed with the special edition, platinum masterpiece that stared back up at him. Sundae watched him eye the expensive gift with her hands in her lap.

"It's engraved," she said softly.

Quamir pulled the watch out of the box. He looked at the engraving then read it out loud.

"I have loved you since forever," he said in a thick voice clouded with emotion.

A sheet of silence fell over the table. Sundae and Quamir locked eyes and at that moment, the past didn't matter. All that mattered was that they had somehow connected again. For a moment, Quamir reconsidered his plan. However, he knew that if he didn't go through with it, he would forever be the side nigga to Sundae and he couldn't have that. Not when he was used to having all of her.

He got up from his seat after putting his watch on and walked over to her. He grabbed his face and looked down at her. He pecked her lips until she slipped her tongue into his mouth. They kissed fervently until Sundae started to cry. Quamir pulled back and wiped her tears away.

"Stop stressing, bae. Everything will work out how it's supposed to. I love my gift, and I love you. I mean a nigga love you for real," he said and kissed her again.

Sundae smiled and he went back to his seat. Quamir put his box away as the servers brought out their meals. They blessed the food and Sundae watched him eat.

"So how is Darby doing? How's the baby?" Her question came out nicely, but Quamir was no fool. He knew that Sundae was way past hot at him about Darby possibly being pregnant by him.

"She cool," he said and ate some of his salad.

Sundae nodded with pursed lips. "So did she get you a gift yet? You still fucking her? What's up?" she asked.

Sundae knew she wasn't right, but Quamir made her possessive. She did not like the idea of him being with Darby.

"Ma, we having a good time. I don't call and spazz out on you because you with your husband. You should show me the same respect," he said calmly.

Sundae rolled her eyes at him. "Just tell me this, Quamir. Do you love her?"

Quamir looked at Sundae as if she had lost her mind. He chuckled at the nerve that she had. "You a real piece of work, Sundae. I'm not about to keep explaining this shit to you because I don't have to," he said angrily tired of her games.

"Oh, you don't?"

Quamir looked at her. "Nah, I fucking don't, and if you don't stop doing this shit then we can call this little bullshit ass friendship we got quits. I'm tired of arguing with you about Darby. That ain't my bitch and on some real shit my situation with her ain't got shit to do with you," he said being brutally honest with her.

Sundae tucked her bottom lip into her mouth as her eyes watered. They were just having a good time, but she was now ready to go. Quamir ignored her pouting and continued to eat his food. Sundae eventually gave in to the enticing aromas that were lifting off of her plate. She started eating and it was Quamir's turn to watch her. He was pissed at how she fucked up their date, but her jealousy did turn him on. The only way to put it was that they were a toxic love, but neither was ready to give the other completely up.

"Hopefully, that food calms your mean ass down some. You know I only love you," he told her.

Sundae smiled and swallowed her food. She didn't wanna take it there but being as though it was just them two she did. "I only love you too," she said speaking a truth that she had been thinking for years.

Quamir looked at her with an intense gaze. "I already knew that, ma. Finish your food," he said and she started back eating.

****

"Happy Birthday, nigga," Qwote said and patted Quamir's shoulder.

Quamir smiled. He was beyond fucked up. He and Frenchie had been smoking all day. He leaned against the counter in Darby's upscale cabin feeling like a million bucks. He'd spent a good date with Sundae getting in some quality time at the restaurant, and now he was chilling with his family. He was good. Darby had hit him off with some superb head making him feel super relaxed.

"Thank you. Ain't this shit fly, nigga?" He asked his brother and looked around.

Qwote and Lourdes looked around the two story cabin impressed. It was nice and again they wondered just how much money Darby's ass had. The cabin was laid out with 60inch TV's, new furniture, and even a Jacuzzi on the second-floor balcony.

"Yeah this is really nice," Lourdes said never one to hate.

"Why thank you all. I've had this place for a year now," Darby said walking up.

She walked up on Quamir and kissed him sensually making everyone look at them. Quamir often downplayed his fling with Darby.

"I see you," Qwote said giving his brother the eye.

Darby decided to slowly suck on Quamir's bottom lip and poke her ass out.

This could be you but you playing. Standing over there with Lourdes' wide body ass.

"Alright, girl, cool out," Quamir said not liking the show she was putting on in front of his people. He also didn't want Lourdes to run back to Sundae with some shit to tell her.

"Um, okay, baby. Lourdes, can I show you and our Qwote here to your bedroom?" she asked wiping her lips.

Lourdes looked at Darby. She did not appreciate the way Darby worded the question. "Yes, you can show me and my man to our room," she said.

Frenchie laughed from the living room. "Darby, you better chill out. Lourdes don't play that shit," he said and went back to watching his game.

Darby looked at Lourdes. They were both rocking the short hair. Lourdes had a small gold ball in her nose that Darby hadn't seen before. She made a note of it to make sure she went and got one. Lourdes was also wearing a few David Yurman bracelets stacked on top of one another. Darby made sure to check them out so that she could buy them as well.

"Lourdes, I'm trying to be nice here. I really want us to start over. I didn't mean anything by that comment either," she said nicely.

Plus, he's my nigga any fucking way, Darby said to herself. Lourdes stared at her for a moment before shrugging.

"I guess. So yeah you can show us where the room is at," she said.

Darby smiled and led the way making sure to switch hard. Qwote did check it out, but he wasn't impressed. Darby's ass wasn't even close to being as big as Lourdes' ass.

"Well here it is," Darby said taking them into a spacious room that had a queen sized bed in the middle of the floor.

Lourdes looked around while Qwote dropped their bags onto the floor. "This is really nice. We can take it from here, though," Qwote said.

Darby nodded and slowly walked out of the room. Darby went into the bathroom that was in her and Quamir's bedroom and she shut the door. She pulled out her iPad that was in one of her bags and logged into the security system online that she had for her cabin. Immediately the screens popped up, and she was able to see what was going on in all of the rooms. Darby smiled giddily to herself.

She tapped onto the screen that was Qwote and Lourdes' room, and was pissed when she realized she needed to be on her computer to hear them. Darby was, however, able to still watch them. She rocked her leg nervously as she watched Qwote pull Lourdes into his arms. They spoke to one another for a moment before they started kissing. Their kiss was so intense it brought tears to Darby's eyes. Qwote quickly dispersed of Lourdes' shirt and then her bra. Darby let out a whale of a cry as she watched Qwote bend his head to pull Lourdes' hard nipple into his mouth.

"That bitch ass nigga!" she hissed with her nails digging into the screen of the iPad.

Darby could see the pleasure that was etched on Lourdes' face as Qwote took her down to the ground. He quickly took off her pants and then her underwear. Darby slowly shook her head knowing what was next.

"Baby, please don't do it…. please don't," she pleaded with angry tears sliding down her cheeks.

Qwote climbed between Lourdes' legs and while staring her in the eyes stuck his face into her vagina. Darby's chest caved in as if she was shot. She tossed her iPad into the tub as hard as she could, making the screen shatter completely. Darby then tossed two large candles into the wall. She grabbed a huge shard of glass and pressed it against the vein inside of her left wrist.

"How could he? Why? God, if you exist you wouldn't have let this happen to me. I have done nothing to deserve this life. He is my fucking man," she said, saying the last part through gritted teeth.

Quamir rushed into the bathroom and looked at her then the iPad. He watched her tears roll down her face as he eyed her holding the glass to her wrist. His eyes nearly bulged out of his head.

"Darby, what the fuck are you doing?" he asked.

Darby looked up at him with blurred vision. She was so hurt. She wanted to grab her gun from out of her bag and shoot the shit out of Lourdes. Right between her eyes was where she would plant the bullets. Darby pressed the glass into her skin welcoming the pain. Anything to take her mind away from the betrayal that she had just witnessed was fine with her.

"I can't do this anymore, Quamir. I'm ready to die," she confessed.

Quamir took a slow step towards her, and she cut her wrist just enough to make herself bleed.

"Stay the fuck away from me! Please just let me do this. Please, I wanna die," she whined.

Quamir shook his head. He was way too high to assess the situation.

"Aye, Lourdes, come here! Lourdes!" he yelled. He looked at Darby and exhaled. "Look, whatever you going through we can fix. You pregnant and you trying to kill yourself? What type of shit is you on?" he asked looking her up and down.

Darby looked at Quamir angrily. "All you fucking care about is this baby? You don't even love me do you?" she asked.

Quamir stared at her not sure what to say. Lourdes and Qwote walked up to him and he sighed. He was happy to have back up.

"Oh my god, Darby, what are you doing?" she asked.

Darby didn't even look at Lourdes as she pressed the glass harder into her skin. She looked at Qwote and noted that he was dressed casually in black basketball shorts with a black beater and black Gucci flip-flops. She thought back on him using his tongue to service Lourdes and she cried harder.

"My brother just told me that my mom is on crack," she said reciting the first thing she could think of.

"Damn," Qwote said looking at her. He didn't like Darby but he felt for her. He stepped into the bathroom and approached her. Qwote wasn't trying to take over, but naturally he was a leader, so it was always easy for him to take over a situation. He gently grabbed the glass from Darby and bent down so that they were eye level.

"Look, I don't know what it feels like to have someone you love so much be addicted to that shit, but I know it's gotta hurt. What you can't do is hurt yourself because of that.

You have a baby to think about now. Put your child's welfare before your own. I better not ever see you doing no shit like this again," he said and Darby slowly nodded. Qwote pulled her into his arms, and she cried into his chest.

"I know I'm just so hurt. I mean she'd already been sick then for her to be on drugs just baffles me. How reckless could she be? I feel like I have no one," she said into his shirt.

Qwote rubbed her back feeling like she was in dire need of a mental evaluation.

"Don't think that. As long as you carrying my brother's baby you gon' be good. You got way too much shit to be blessed about, girl. Stop tripping and let's get you cleaned up then we'll finish enjoying Quamir's birthday," he told her with finality in his voice.

Darby nodded and Qwote helped her stand. He walked her over to the sink and looked at Quamir.

"Help her, nigga," he said making Quamir step away from Lourdes and join them at the sink.

Quietly Lourdes watched Darby get cleaned up with a million things running through her head. As much as she hated what Darby did, she couldn't help but to feel bad for her. Darby was definitely going through some things, and Lourdes wasn't sure if pushing her away was the best thing. She felt like Darby was in need of a true friend, and that just maybe she could look past the club incident and be there for her.

The minute Darby returned from Quamir's birthday weekend at the cabin, she went to visit her dealer Tevin. She'd spent two days with Qwote soaking up as much attention from him as she could. All it did was make her even more excited to get Lourdes out of the picture. She felt like a new woman with nothing but sweet old revenge on her mind as she sat next to him.

"Hey so how many people have you robbed?"

The young handsome man looked Darby up and down and smirked. She was far too beautiful to be so ruthless. "I robbed three people in the vicinity like you asked me to. Now, what's up?"

Darby went into her bag and pulled out some money. She handed it to him, and he placed it in his middle car console. His hand went to Darby's thigh and she smiled at him.

"I can't suck you today. I have some bad morning sickness. Your nut might make me throw up. But look, I've been thinking I might need for you to handle somebody permanently for me," she said.

The young man's eyes looked her over before he looked straight ahead. "Ma, please tell me what happened?"

Darby sighed dramatically. "They pissed me off. I think they need to just fucking die," she ranted envisioning the people she wanted dead.

Tevin chuckled. "Nah I'm saying what happened to you? Why you so fucking angry, shorty? Who made you like this?" he asked. "Like why you so angry? Were you raped or beat as a kid? What the fuck made you so corrupt?" he asked just having to know. In Tevin's eyes people usually went through something in order for them to be demented. He wanted to know why Darby was so volatile.

Darby pushed his hand away suddenly in a bad mood. "Who made me like this? Wow, ain't this some shit. A fucking low life, drug peddling, crack dealer is judging me. Nigga, you sell drugs three houses down from a fucking middle school, you gutter rat ass nigga. What made you that way? Huh?" She asked glaring at him.

SLAP! SLAP! SLAP!

"Bitch, I let a lot of shit slide because you can suck a mean dick, but don't you ever use them big motherfucking soup coolers of yours to talk to me like that again. I'll kill your ass, and I'm sure no one but the tricks and johns will miss you. Get the fuck out of my car and call me when you got your mind right," he said coolly.

Darby held her face. He'd slapped her so hard her mouth was bleeding. She slowly got out of the car and walked over to her truck. As she got in she contemplated how she would handle him. Would she set him up to get robbed or taken to jail, or would she let his slaps slide because she needed him?

"I'll use his ass until I don't need him then I'm having that bitch set up to be knocked. His sexy ass gon' be somebody's bitch very soon," she said and started her car up.

Darby drove to her doctor's office and parked in the first available spot. She cleaned her face up before going in. She was surprised to see Quamir's mother sitting inside of the waiting room waiting for her. Aida wasn't too sure how she felt about Darby, but what she did know was that she was ecstatic to be an expectant grandmother. She was going to be there for Darby until Darby gave her a reason not to.

Darby signed in then went to sit next to Aida. Aida smiled lovingly at her and grabbed Darby's small hand.

"Darby, I came because I want to experience all that I can concerning the baby. I'ma grown woman as you are and woman to woman I need for you to tell me. Is there a chance my son isn't the father? If there is, I will still be there because he has a fifty, fifty chance but I just need to know. I don't play games when it comes to my sons. They're all I have, sweetie, and I would die for them, so woman to woman were you messing with any other men besides my Quamir?" she asked making sure to look Darby in the eye.

Darby shook her head quickly. She was low-key pissed at Aida for coming at her in such a way, but she knew to play it cool. After all, Aida was the woman that had blessed her with Qwote.

"No there isn't, Ma. I promise Quamir is the father of this baby," she replied.

Aida smiled with relief. She wanted to discuss the whole "ma" thing with Darby, but she just decided to let it go. Quamir had told her he would handle it, but he obviously hadn't.

"Okay good well let's see how my grandbaby is doing," Aida said and sat back.

Darby smiled at her despite being irritated. If she didn't love Qwote so much she would surely have whooped Aida's ass. Darby decided to browse Qwote's work email that she had hacked into while waiting on her name to be called. Once inside the doctor's room they were told the baby was fine and to return in six weeks. Darby then took Aida out to eat and was more than surprised to see that Qwote, Quamir, and Lourdes were waiting in the restaurant for them. Quamir gave Darby half a hug then warmly hugged his mother. Darby hugged Lourdes who she had had a good time with at the cabin then she walked up on Qwote. Just his scent sent her body into overload. He smelled delicious and looked even better in a slate gray suit with a black shirt and black shoes. His watch with the diamond bezel was blinding every eye it hit then his smile creamed every panty in the vicinity.

Darby looked at him like he was a prized possession. The winning lotto ticket while Qwote looked at her with pity. He felt like she was fifty shades of fucked up. He wasn't sure what his brother was going to do if the baby was his, because Qwote knew that Darby had some serious fucking issues.

"What's up, Darby?" He asked giving her a hug.

Darby hugged him a little tight before letting him go. She looked up into his eyes and smiled.

"I'm good. I'm currently trying to get my mom some help. I really appreciate everything you did for me at the cabin," she said staring him in the eyes.

Qwote stroked his beard while smiling at her. "That's what's up. I'm praying for her too," he said.

"Yes, honey, we all are," Aida said walking up on them and grabbing her hand.

Darby hit Aida with a strained smile. *Bitch, if you interrupt me and my man again, I'ma have your ass killed,* Darby thought. She looked back at Qwote and watched him walk up on Lourdes and wrap his arms around her waist. Darby sighed and looked down at the floor. Aida noticed her mood change and looked at Quamir, whose face was buried in his phone. She took Darby over to him and grabbed his phone. Aida put it in her purse and smiled lovingly while looking up at him.

"Tend to your future child's mother," she said and gently pushed Darby into him.

Quamir opened his mouth to protest and Aida shot him a stern look. He may have been a grown man, but she was still his mother and her word was law.

Chapter Fourteen

Lourdes was packing up more clothes to give away when she heard a knock at the door. She went to check it and was extremely surprised to see Frenchie standing there. She opened the door for him and he stepped in. Frenchie walked through the hallway and into her family room. He got comfortable on her sofa as she looked at him curiously.

"Qwote isn't here."

Frenchie nodded and removed his Gucci sunglasses from his slanted eyes. He looked at Lourdes and swallowed hard. He wasn't sure what brought him to her place. He knew that Qwote was in Ann Arbor in a meeting. He knew that Lourdes was home, and he felt like they needed to talk but now he wasn't so sure. He felt beyond fucked up for feeling how he did, especially because he knew that Lourdes didn't feel the same. She'd made that clear in New York.

"I know. I just talked to him," he replied.

Lourdes shook her head. She walked over to the opposite sofa and sat down. She looked at Frenchie. She knew that just talking with him like that in such a private setting was wrong. She as very uncomfortable with the situation.

"Fred, we can't have this talk again."

Frenchie stared at her for a moment. Lourdes was beautiful but it wasn't like she was the baddest. The reality was there was always somebody who looked better than the next person. No, Lourdes was everything to him because he'd known her most of his life, and he'd watched her blossom into this woman that he wanted. That he dreamed about and that he often tried to copy.

"I know. Look that shit that happened in New York was foul, and I know that I fucked up. I appreciate you not telling Qwote."

"Okay, then why are you here?" Lourdes asked nervously.

Frenchie sat up and licked his lips. He looked Lourdes in the eyes and he had to say it. Shit if he didn't he was going to fucking go crazy.

"I'm here because I love you. Lolo, I been loving you since you hooked up with my boy. I know this shit is wrong! I love that nigga like a brother. Fuck I know this shit would gut him, but I'm suffering too. Just watching you two together fucks me up. That's the whole reason why I fucking moved to Atlanta. Now that I'm back it's like all I can think about is you. I have to know is there a chance we could be together? If not, I swear on my momma I will let this shit go," he said.

Lourdes stared at Frenchie. He was handsome. Unlike Qwote, Frenchie wasn't versatile. With him, you got what you saw. He was street all day, but he was living good off of music industry money. Frenchie got attention everywhere he went because of his light skin and exotic looks. He was black and his family was creole. He had a reddish tint to his light skin with his dark eyes and a full set of lips. He had a beard with a low cut fade and neatly lined facial hair. He always smelled good. He was tall, and he was also a medium build. He was a good dude too but he wasn't *Qwote*. What happened in New York could never happen again, or Lourdes would have to tell Qwote to ensure that Frenchie stayed away from her.

"Fred, words fail me when I speak on Qwote. That man feeds my soul and is the blood that pumps through my heart. If you knew how much I loved him, you would feel foolish for even being here. I will take my last breath on this earth loving that man. He's my best friend, my lover, my nigga, my therapist, and my king. Soon he will be my husband. What I pray is that you find a woman that loves you the way that I love him," she said sincerely and stood up.

Frenchie whistled as he felt emotions creep up into him that choked him up. *Damn*. Who could ever hear the one they love speak of another that way? Frenchie did feel foolish at that moment. He knew Lourdes meant well and as a man of his word, he stood up and accepted it. He walked up on Lourdes and leaned towards her. He kissed her cheek while touching her hip which in turn made her jump.

"I respect that shit. I mean... we could have been something great," he whispered to her before leaving out of the room.

Lourdes exhaled as she heard him close the door. She sat down on the edge of the sofa and was about to return to packing up her boxes when her house phone rung. She grabbed it.

"Hello."

"Lourdes! I'm having the baby," Sundae yelled before ending the call.

Lourdes rushed to grab her things as her heart raced from the excitement of her about to meet her godchild. She rushed to get into her car and drove as fast as she could to get to the hospital. She called Qwote and he picked up after a few rings.

"What up, sexy?"

"Qwote, Sundae is having the baby," she said excitedly.

"Oh shit, that's what's up. Text me the hospital and I'll fall through. I appreciate that lunch you sent me to *Mi Amor*," he said smiling.

"The lunch? What are you talking about?" Lourdes asked rushing to get to the freeway.

Qwote looked at the phone and frowned. He put it back to his ear and chuckled. Somebody was playing games with him but he wasn't worried.

"Nothing, ma. Text me the details and I'll be up there," he said before ending the call.

Lourdes put her phone away a little irritated. "Who the fuck sending him lunch and shit?" she asked herself out loud. "Yeah, okay," she said. Fifteen minutes later she arrived at the hospital. Lourdes found a spot and rushed in. After finding Sundae's room. She went in and was welcomed by Drama and his mother along with Sundae's mother. Lourdes spoke to everyone before going to her best friend.

Sundae looked a hot mess as she struggled through a contraction. She, however, wasn't yelling or anything. She was taking the pain as best as she could, and Lourdes respected her so much for that. She kissed Sundae's sweaty forehead and smiled at her.

"I'm here, boo. Our baby is on the way," Lourdes said and Sundae managed to smile at her.

"I know. I'm just ready to have it already. This shit hurts," she said as another contraction came.

Lourdes grabbed her hand and held it through another forty-five minutes before Sundae felt the need to push or in her words "shit". Sundae started to push and things seemed to fly by. Zoe Lourdes Howard was born at 8:53 at night, weighing in at six pounds and five ounces. She was gorgeous and everyone was already in love with her. Lourdes felt so honored for her goddaughter to share her name. She vowed to always love and be there for her.

As Lourdes cradled a now cleaned up Zoe she stared down at her. Her eyes watered at the beauty in her arms. She couldn't help but to wonder what her child with Qwote would look like. She kissed the baby's head that was covered with a small furry pink beanie and Lourdes rocked her until she went to sleep. Lourdes stayed at the hospital late into the morning. She walked into her home tired and ready to fall into her bed.

"Fuck you been at?"

Lourdes took off her UGGs and looked at Qwote. He was sitting in his favorite chair in the living room watching *Dead*

Presidents. He was rocking a beater with some sexy ass underwear that were black with a red band around the top. His dick was soft but still the imprint was big.

"The hospital," Lourdes said as she went to their bedroom.

Qwote jumped up and went after her. He followed her into the bedroom. "Then why didn't you answer the fucking phone? You told me you were going to text me the hospital that she was at. You know I don't know her nigga's number," he said.

Lourdes started to take off her clothes. She knew that the whole baby thing was getting old but still it hurt her. She wanted kids and at times, it was hard to front. She'd held Zoe, and all she could do was think about what it would be like to experience something so life changing. She loved Qwote that was without a doubt and she knew he loved her, but she felt that she should also have a say in the way their life went.

"Qwote, I got caught up in everything that was happening and I forgot. Hell, I thought you would have hooked up with the person that sent you some lunch today," she said flippantly.

Qwote snatched Lourdes up by the back of her neck and spun her around. "Say that shit again for me?" he said through gritted teeth.

Not ready to back down Lourdes glared at him. "You heard what the fuck I said, Quinton."

"Aye, you tripping for real. I don't have time for this shit," he said looking down at her.

"Neither do I so get the hell out of my face."

Qwote smirked and grabbed her face. He made her look up at him with a firm grip on her face. "Ma, we have our fair share of problems, but a bitch ain't never been one of them, so don't ever come at me like that again," he said and pushed her head away from him.

Lourdes took a step back and her eyes watered. It wasn't because she was afraid of him no, it was because she was just tired. Tired of pretending to be okay with not having a kid and not being married. Qwote's hard demeanor softened. The only thing that could ever bring him to his knees was Lourdes. His *amor*.

"Ma...talk to me," he said picking her up.

Qwote sat down on the bed with Lourdes on his lap. She looked him in the eyes and slowly shook her head. He gave her a stern look already knowing what was wrong. He touched her stomach gently and her heart fluttered.

"Lourdes, kids are a blessing but so is this. What we got nobody has. I'ma fall back on some of the shit that I'm doing, so that I could take better care of you. Obviously, a nigga slacking if all you can think about is what we don't have. After my next big meeting, we going to Miami to chill for a weekend."

Lourdes smiled. "Qwote, you have work and I'll be good," she lied.

Qwote chuckled. "Shit, you not about to walk around this bitch mad at me, because you done been around Sundae and that baby. We might not be at the point they at, but we got a lot of shit and I don't ever want you to envy another motherfucka's life. I got you and when I say we gon' be good, I mean that shit literally. *Mi Amor*, we gon' be good. So fix your face and come hop on this dick," he said.

Lourdes giggled and kissed him, she loved him so much and his words were so comforting. They'd appeased her for the moment, but Lourdes couldn't help but to still have that yearning inside of her that she knew only a baby and marriage could fill.

A few days later Lourdes sat with Sundae inside of her bedroom. Lourdes was feeling better and spending as much time as she could with her best friend and god daughter.

"I meant to ask you who did you go to the cabin up north with?" Sundae asked Lourdes.

Lourdes sat her phone down on Sundae's glass mirrored dresser and got onto the king sized bed with her. She looked at her god-baby and smiled. Zoe was latched onto Sundae's nipple and sucking all of the milk out of it that she could get.

"I went up north with everyone for Quamir's birthday. It's been so much going on I didn't get to tell you. Darby threw him a get together at her cabin," Lourdes replied.

Sundae's smile wiped off of her face at the mention of Darby's name. "Oh really. So Quamir was there?"

Lourdes looked at her best friend and laughed. "Um yeah, bitch, it was his party."

Sundae nodded feeling a little betrayed by Quamir. She'd talked to him since Lourdes had been back from the cabin, and he had not mentioned any of that stuff to her.

"What's crazy is that Darby tried to kill herself, Sundae," Lourdes said no longer smiling

"She what? What the fuck is wrong with that crazy bitch?"

Lourdes shook her head. "I guess her mom is on crack. She was in the bathroom with some glass to her wrist. Qwote had to calm her down. I felt so bad for her because she is really going through some shit."

"Umph," Sundae said not feeling any remorse for Darby.

Lourdes looked at her friend. She could tell something was going on with her. "Sundae, what's wrong? I know you not feeling Darby like that anymore, but it seems like it's more than that. Babe, talk to me," she said getting worried.

Sundae shook her head as her eyes watered. How could she explain to her friend just how fucked up her life was? Friends shared everything but some stuff you just didn't want anyone to know. Sundae wasn't ready to see the pity in Lourdes' eyes when she revealed her truths.

"Nothing, I'm just so tired. Drama is already working again spending long hours in the studio, and I'm just emotional. I'll be good," she said and tried to laugh it off.

Lourdes stared at Sundae for a second before leaning towards her. She kissed Sundae on the cheek and tugged on the end of one of her coils.

"We're sisters, boo. Don't front for me. If you wanna cry, then fucking cry. Shit, I cried the other day thinking about you," she expressed sitting back.

"Why did you cry thinking about me?"

Lourdes shrugged. "I wish I had a husband and a baby. I thought about all of the good things you've been blessed with and I cried. I'm so proud of the woman you are. The salon you own, that fine ass man you got, and this beautiful ass baby. You have it all, Sundae. You living the dream, girl, and I'm happy for you," she said and truly meant it.

Sundae looked at Lourdes speechless. *If you only knew, Lourdes,* she thought.

"Thank you but no one's life is perfect, Lourdes, and mines damn sure isn't. I love Zoe, but I do miss when I had that freedom that you do. You and Qwote can do so much shit right now without restrictions. I don't have that luxury anymore. I now have another life to consider. Enjoy the relationship while it's just you two, Lourdes."

Lourdes nodded and looked down at Zoe. She was enjoying her man, but still that nagging feeling that something was missing was still there.

Chapter Fifteen

"Darby, we've been expecting you," Diana said nervously.

Darby stepped into the living room and sat her bag onto her mother's coffee table. She stared at her older brother as he stood before her in his expensive suit and shoes with a smug look on his handsome, chocolate face. Darby hated her brother and the feeling was mutual. They'd never been nice to one another.

"Yeah, we have. I been talking to Mom, and I think it's time to try again with rehab. Have you been condoning her doing this shit, Darby?" he asked.

Darby went over to the chair and sat down. She'd had a long morning because one of her clients wanted to do anal so her ass was extra sore, and she had only went to her mother's because Diana said it was an emergency. Darby was hoping she was overdosing or something. The last thing she expected was to see her only sibling.

"Of course I haven't, *Daren*," she said snidely.

Daren looked at Darby and frowned. She was not his most favorite person in the world, but he did still love her. "Have you been on your meds?"

Diana's eyes darted to Darby's nervously. Her medicine was a topic that no one brought up; however, Daren wasn't afraid of Darby or her tirades.

"Daren, the quickest way for me to fuck you up is for you to bring that bullshit up. I don't need medicine!" she yelled getting emotional. She sat up ready to go at it with him. "I didn't need medicine when you all let me sleep on the fucking street! Or when a no good ass pimp had me turning tricks. I didn't need those bullshit ass pills then, so I damn sure don't need them now. Nothing is wrong with me!" She yelled.

Diana jumped up. She walked up to Daren and looked up at him. "Please, just drop it," she muttered.

Daren looked around her and at Darby, who was now rocking herself slowly while mumbling obscenities up under her breath. He looked at his mother. He wasn't sure how, but he had been born into one fucked up ass family. The minute his father passed away, his good wholesome family fell apart.

"Mom, she's got a lot of issues and she needs to be on that medicine. You didn't forget what she did to The Harrison's did you?" he asked.

Diana's eyes watered. She thought back briefly on how Darby had ruined the lives of the people that once lived down the street from them. The young girl had befriended Darby, and they quickly became best friends. Darby became obsessed with the girl's dad and accused him of raping her. The whole thing caused a huge case, and he was eventually sentenced to five years in jail. Darby later came out and changed up the story, but Diana was so embarrassed by the whole ordeal she never told the judge. The father had only been released for a few years, and of course his wife had long ago moved off of the block. Diana had Darby evaluated and they diagnosed her with being manic depressant and paranoid schizophrenic. She was supposed to take medicine daily. Darby had been off of her meds for years. Some days she was okay and some days she really wasn't.

"Of course, I didn't. Look let's just discuss this rehab stuff while she is here. I need the support from you all," she said and they both sat down.

Daren cleared his throat. "Okay well, I've found Mom a rehab facility to go to. She will be there for six months, and I would like for you to help me pay for it," he said.

Darby smiled. "You have got to be fucking kidding me. I'm already paying all of the bills over here. You have a good job, you can pay for that shit. I'm not doing it."

Daren shook his head. He was trying his best to be cordial with Darby, but she was pushing him. He knew a lot more about her than Diana did when it came to how she made her money. Sadly, some of his colleagues had used her services. Daren felt a level of hatred for her, because of how she was degrading herself.

"Bitch, I know you got the fucking money. You stay on your back," he said angrily.

Darby grabbed the remote and threw it at him effectively hitting him in the head. He touched the tender spot it hit and glared at her.

"I should beat your ass," he said through gritted teeth.

"She's pregnant, Daren," Diana told him.

163

"Yes, I'm pregnant and if you touch me I promise Qwote will fuck you up," Darby said still pissed at the words he'd spoken to him.

"Qwote," Daren mumbled thinking that the name sounded familiar. Daren shrugged not knowing the name.

Darby looked at her mother as she slipped her purse onto her shoulder.

"I wish you the best of luck. If you need me for *anything* call me," she said and walked away.

Darby left her mother's home and decided to stalk Lourdes. Her fixation with Lourdes was one she couldn't let go just yet. She didn't too much care for Lourdes, but for some reason she loved to be around her. She liked to watch her talk and see the types of food she ate, because Darby knew that she would soon be with Qwote. She wanted to remind him of Lourdes so that he didn't go back to her.

Darby already had Lourdes' hairstyle, but she felt like she could definitely have more things in common with her. She logged into Lourdes Find My iPhone account and saw that Lourdes was at Oakland Mall. She smiled and headed that way. She decided to listen to Lourdes' voicemails on her speaker as she drove.

"Hey, *Mi Amor*, it's me. I'm stuck in the Chi doing work. I'll be back home late. Don't get to tripping. Oh and the way you were sucking on a nigga this morning had me smiling all damn day. Guess who got some diamonds coming they way? I love you, girl," Qwote said.

Darby wanted to erase the message, but it had already been saved so she skipped past it and let the next one play.

"What up? True to my word I let that shit go *but*...my mom was asking about you since I'm always bringing you up. It's not looking too good for her, Lolo. Can you come through? Let me know," Frenchie said.

Darby ended the voicemail call with a huge grin on her face. "Now Fred why the fuck is you calling that hoe? You didn't wanna fuck me, but you checking for her? I can't wait to let my honey know about this," Darby said giggling.

It took Darby thirty minutes to make it to the mall. She walked around until she spotted Lourdes coming out of a shoe store. Darby noticed how Lourdes walked with sort of a strut. Darby's ass wasn't big like Lourdes' so she couldn't completely mimic her walk, but she could recreate it. She also noticed that Lourdes let her bag rest in the crook of her arm and sort of swing when she walked. Darby did her purse the same way as she walked up on her.

"Hey, Lourdes!"

Lourdes stopped walking and turned around. She gave Darby a once over and smiled. After the cabin, they had been cordial to one another. Lourdes hadn't forgotten about what happened at the club, but she was trying to let it go. She could tell that Darby really needed a friend.

"Hey. How are you? How is the baby?" She asked and looked at Darby's stomach.

"We're good. I can't believe I seen you here. Do you wanna shop and talk?"

Lourdes smiled. "I'm being cordial with you, but I'm not sure if we're back at the point where we can hang solo and shit," she replied being honest.

Darby was surprised by Lourdes' response. "Lourdes," Darby grabbed her stomach that was starting to form a small pudge. "I promise you I had no idea Palma would do any of that including the video. I gave you all of the info I knew on her. That's why she's on the run. Can we please start over? I'm going through so much shit right now, and I'm in desperate need of a real friend," she begged, so tired of kissing Lourdes' ass.

This bitch better answer correctly, Darby thought giving Lourdes a sullen look.

"Darby…" Lourdes sighed and shrugged her shoulders. "Fine; look I swear the minute some shit doesn't go right with us I'm completely done with you," she said giving her a serious look.

Darby nodded smiling. They hugged and Darby sniffed her neck. Lourdes pulled back laughing. "Girl, what the hell you sniffing me for?"

They started to walk and Darby laughed to play it off. "Girl, I love perfume. Is that Bond No. 9?"

Lourdes shook her head as she received a call from Frenchie. "Nope, it isn't."

"Chanel? Jadore Dior? Escada? Chloe?" Darby called off eager to know the brand.

Lourdes sent Frenchie to voicemail not really paying attention to Darby's questions. "It's Issey Miyake," she said and Darby quickly stored the information in her head.

While they walked and talked Darby was able to find out what Lourdes' favorite color was. She learned about the different foods that Lourdes liked to cook, and that Qwote's favorite dish was lasagna.

"So have you made up with Sundae?" Lourdes asked as they walked into the lingerie store.

"No, not yet. She seems angrier with me than you do. I mean, if I didn't know any better I would say she's jealous because, I'm with Quamir, which is crazy, because she's with Drama right?" Darby said and laughed.

Lourdes laughed with her, wondering if that was the case. Even if it was she would never admit it to Darby. "Right, Sundae is not thinking about Quamir's ass. Let's finish shopping," Lourdes said brushing it off.

Darby followed after her smirking. Every piece of lingerie Lourdes picked up she did as well, she just got it in another color. She was determined to be like Lourdes, but ten times better so that Qwote would be more than satisfied with her.

Chapter Sixteen

"I can't believe I'm doing this shit," Sundae said as she got out of her car.

"Well, you here now. How you feeling?" Quamir asked walking up on her.

Sundae looked up into his eyes. Her daughter was with her mother. Drama was in New York working on a few people's mixtapes and wouldn't be back for a few days. It had been a month since she'd had her baby, and sadly she had been counting down the time to see Quamir

"I'm okay. I'm still mad as hell at you," she said and stepped around him.

Quamir chuckled as they walked up his driveway. Quamir owned a beautiful home in Palmer Park. It was just him so he loved his privacy. For that reason alone, Darby had never been invited to his home, although unbeknownst to him she did know where he stayed at. She also knew about his rental property that he sometimes used for his freaks.

"Sundae, I already told you that I didn't know about that cabin bullshit. Don't come over here trying to argue with a nigga," he said following her into the house.

Sundae rolled her eyes. "Whatever, you so full of sh—"

"I'm full of what?" Quamir asked walking up behind her and wrapping his arms around her waist. Sundae closed her eyes as he closed the door with his foot, and set the alarm with his left hand. "Let's go upstairs," he said quietly.

Sundae debated over if she was doing the right thing as she went up the stairs. His place was once like a home to her. She'd missed being there but, more importantly, she missed Quamir. They hadn't had sex in three years. Sundae was so nervous she didn't know what to do.

"Qua…"

"Shhhh…baby, I waited. This is our time," he said silencing her.

Sundae nodded with tears in her eyes. Although she loved Quamir more than she loved Drama, she still felt fucked up for cheating. Drama was a good man. He was also a great father; he just wasn't what she thought he would be. He actually worked way more than Quamir did, leaving her a lot of time to be lonely and think about Quamir.

"Don't do that, come here," Quamir said.

Sundae was a nervous wreck as Quamir pulled her over to the bed and began to strip her down. He kissed the back of her shoulder and walked away so that he could turn off the bedroom light and cut on some music. The only light that illuminated the bedroom was from the adjoining bathroom door that was halfway open. Sundae sat on the bed, naked, and nervous as Usher's sweet voice crooned through the speakers.

'Now we gon' do this thing a little different tonight. You gon' come over pick me up in your ride. You gon' knock and then you gon' wait. Ooh u gon' take me on a date...'

Quamir's soft lips pulled Sundae out of her thoughts, away from the music and brought her back to the present. She looked up into Quamir's eyes and he smiled at her. He was naked. His man was standing at full attention, and Sundae was mixed with a few emotions with the biggest one being excitement.

"Lay back. I wanna tie you up," he said and licked his lips.

Sundae heart nearly leaped from her chest. "Qua..."

"Just do it, ma," Quamir said cutting her off.

Sundae nodded and laid back on the bed. Quamir used his expensive ties to tie Sundae to his headboard that was made specifically for that. Before they'd split up they often did role playing and things of that nature. It wasn't uncommon for him to tie her up. Quamir kissed Sundae on the cheek then sensually kissed her on the lips after he tied her up. Sundae squirmed as he started to suck on her puckered nipples.

"Ohhh...Quamir...," she moaned.

Quamir pulled her nipples into his mouth and he sucked hard. He pulled back when he tasted her breast milk and went to the other nipple. His hand slowly slid down her body, and he found her sex. He stuck three fingers inside of her and started to slowly finger her until her breathing became labored. Sundae quickly climaxed and Quamir climbed between her legs, and slid on a condom before he slowly inched himself inside of her. Sundae's eyes watered and her tears slowly escaped her eyes as he filled her up. It was the greatest pleasure she'd ever experienced. She began to get wrapped up into Quamir and their lovemaking as he put it on her.

"Damn I missed this shit," he said sliding in and out of her.

Sundae gazed up at him completely lost in the moment. "I did too," she moaned.

Quamir licked his lips and hiked her leg up. He sat up on his knees and used her calves as support as he rocked in and out of her. Sundae's mouth fell open and her stomach contracted. Quamir wasn't a little man. His dick was giving her pain and pleasure. She pulled against the restraint wishing she could push him back just a little. He smiled at her and hit it harder.

"Nah, you gon' take this dick, baby. This still my shit ain't it?" he asked.

Sundae looked at him as he slowed his movements. Quamir began to slowly slide in and out of her. Every time he slid in he made sure to go all the way to the back of her pussy. Sundae's body quivered. He was fucking her mercilessly.

"Yes…damn yes," she surrendered.

Quamir's dick grew even harder at her admission. He pushed her legs even further back and started to pound in and out of her.

"Do he fuck you like this? Do he fill that pussy up like I do?" he asked in and groaned at how wet she was.

Sundae shook her head, but it wasn't good enough. He needed to hear her say it. He let one of her legs go so that he could show her clitoris some attention. Sundae's body shook. She looked up at him with pleading watery eyes.

"Quamir...please.... slow down," she begged. She could feel a big orgasm coming and she was afraid to let it take over. Quamir ignored her as he slid deep within her.

"Nah fuck that. Is he fucking you like this? Tell me," he demanded and pinched her clitoris.

Sundae's back arched off of the bed. Her vision blurred and she started to cum. "No! He doesn't!" she shouted.

Quamir groaned and let go of her clitoris. He fucked her through her climax and then filled the condom. Quamir and Sundae fucked for hours before passing out in his bed without a care in the world.

A few days later Sundae sat with her mother in her parents' home. She was so sore she didn't know what to do. Quamir had been fucking her so good she was thinking about getting a wheelchair for a few days because her legs were like Jell-O.

"You're pushing it."

Sundae kissed Zoe all over her face making Zoe look up at her. Sundae then looked at her mother and smiled.

"I'm sorry what did you say?"

Sundae's mother, Jessica, frowned at her oldest daughter. "I said you're pushing it. You playing with fire, Sundae, and you know it. Leave Quamir alone and act like a wife," she said.

Unlike Lourdes, Sundae was not close to her mother. Her parents had given her a good life, but they just weren't close. With them, it was more about perception than reality. As long as they looked perfect it didn't matter if they were or weren't.

"Mom, I really don't know what you're talking about," Sundae said and grabbed her cell phone. She checked to see if she had any missed calls or texts from Quamir. Jessica watched her with an unsatisfied look on her face.

"That's what I'm talking about. All week you've been leaving Zoe over here with your sister, so you can go creep. And please don't lie because I know you have. I followed you yesterday, and if it was that easy for me then it will be even easier for your husband to figure it out. What the hell is wrong with you, girl? Are you really going to mess up your marriage for him?"

Sundae became so mad her cheeks turned red. She couldn't believe her mother was calling her out.

"I love him. That's something you and Dad know nothing about. I made a mistake when I left him."

Jessica laughed and rolled her eyes. "So this is the way you make that right? By cheating on your husband that cherishes the ground you walk on? I swear this will end badly if you don't end this now. Quamir is a good man. He will be okay, sweetie, so don't worry about that. You did not have to come back here and give him some nookie to make him smile. I'm sure he's been getting some anyways. Are you really that naïve? I mean what the fuck. You chose Draven so deal with it. You have his daughter yet you behave this way? How selfish could you be?" Jessica asked her daughter.

Sundae's mother's judgmental words brought tears to her eyes. She placed Zoe in her bassinet and looked down at her hands. The reason she'd married Drama was because she found herself pregnant again by him, and her parents had threatened to cut her off at the time. She was afraid to not have their financial backing, and she was also looking for love. Drama was attentive back then. He was perfect until she realized that he was no different than Quamir only worse because he actually wasn't Quamir.

"Mom, all you've ever done was tell me what to do. I don't need your money now so I can do whatever the hell I wanna do. I love you, but I don't need your permission to do a damn thing," she said angrily.

Jessica listened to her daughter and nodded. She grabbed her coffee cup and gracefully stood up. She looked at Sundae and wanted to tell her that she knew what it was like to love a man that wasn't your husband. She wanted to tell her that she understood that pain, but that she'd chosen her kids' happiness over her own but she didn't. Jessica felt guilty because she worked so much, so she stayed with her husband long after she had stopped loving him for her kids, but she wasn't Sundae. She would allow for her daughter to make her own mistakes.

"You're absolutely right, Sundae. You don't need my permission to do anything. Whether you believe it or not, I love you, Sundae, and I always have. I will be here to catch you when you fall, sweetie," she said and walked out of the sunroom.

Sundae lifted her head to watch her mother exit the room. Her cell phone rang and Drama's face popped up onto the screen. She felt a huge wave of guilt as she answered his call.

"Hey, baby. How are you?"

"I'm good. Headed back home now. I miss you and that beautiful face. What you and my baby been doing?" he asked.

Sundae had a flashback of Quamir and she shook her head. "Nothing. I've been spending a lot of time at my parents' home."

"Oh okay. Well, I'll be back tonight. I can't wait to see and taste you, baby," he said before ending the call.

Sundae put her phone away and looked at Zoe who was now asleep. Zoe was a reflection of her with snippets of Drama in her. Sundae was so conflicted she didn't know what to do. She did wanna give her family a chance, but she was starting to feel so empty inside. Quamir filled her up and Drama just didn't do it for her. The more she sat down and thought about their relationship, the more she realized that she had never been fully happy with Drama. She felt so bad for even leading him on. She was working off of selfishness, and now she was paying the price.

Sundae touched Zoe's foot and her heart ached.

"What do I do, Zoe? I can't put him over you, and you deserve a chance at having a real family. I have to let him go," she said. Sundae went to her phone and blocked Quamir's cell and work numbers. She put her phone away and sat back on the sectional. She closed her eyes and cried at what she could have had with Quamir, and what would never be.

Chapter Seventeen

"This is so nice," Lourdes said.

Qwote rode next to her on the horse nervously. He was what he considered to be a worldly person, but some shit he felt just wasn't for men. He was uncomfortable as hell on the horse. He moved his package around while trying to watch Lourdes. She was looking so happy and beautiful in her two-piece swimming suit that was shutting South Beach down.

"Yeah it's cool," he said as the horses walked them through the water.

Lourdes smiled at him and blew him a kiss. They horse ride lasted for another fifteen minutes before they went to the shore and got off of them. Qwote adjusted his swim trunks while Lourdes fixed her swimming suit. Qwote walked up behind her and pulled her bottoms out of her ass.

"Gotta make sure my shit covered up," he said and slapped her playfully on the butt.

Lourdes laughed and he grabbed her hand. They walked down the beach headed to no specific destination. Qwote eventually pulled her over to their lounge chairs and they sat down. He gazed at her as she soaked up the sun rays. Lourdes was wearing a black and hot pink two-piece swimming suit, a one-piece body chain on, and aviator shades with her hair slicked back. She looked so damn good to him and every other man that they passed.

"You look good, baby. Are you enjoying yourself?" he asked.

Lourdes smiled at him. "Of course, I am. You know Miami is one of my most favorite places to visit. Are you having fun? Your work phone been blowing up since we been here," she said.

Qwote nodded. "Yeah I'm good. I want us to go out with some people later. One of my clients gave me some tickets to his concert," he said.

"Okay well, who is it?"

Qwote stroked his small beard before replying. "My nigga Kasam."

Lourdes turned away from him and smiled. Kasam was a well-known rapper that was from Detroit like them. She had no idea that Qwote knew him. Qwote watched her grin like a school girl and he shook his head.

"Cut all that bullshit out. That nigga cool *but* he ain't me," he said and they both laughed.

Lourdes leaned over and gave him a juicy kiss on the lips. She looked into his eyes and admired how handsome he was. He was looking extremely sexy in his black swim trunks showing off his ripped body that was decorated with tattoos. Qwote had this prettiness to him that pulled you in, but he was rugged in a lot of ways as well. Lourdes loved everything about him. She touched his cheek and sighed in content.

"I love you, baby," she told him.

Qwote grabbed her face and kissed her breath away before telling her he loved her too.

A few hours later Lourdes and Qwote stood backstage at the Fillmore watching Kasam perform. Lourdes and Qwote were getting looks left and right for being such an attractive couple. Lourdes wore a pink wrap dress with nude platform heels and light makeup. Her hair was curled and she was wearing her David Yurman bangles that she adored. Qwote was on his grown man shit looking very dapper in black slacks with a soft pink Gucci dress shirt that was the same color as Lourdes' dress. He wore his Hublot watch with his diamond pinky ring, and his Louis Vuitton shades. He was smoking on a blunt and talking with Kasam's brother Aamil. Lourdes was standing with Kasam's pregnant wife Erin and Aamil's wife Drew. The ladies smiled at Lourdes admiring her look. They were looking cute as well and Lourdes couldn't help but to notice how fine their men were.

"So are you and Qwote married?" Erin asked her.

Lourdes shook her head while smiling at her. "No not yet," Lourdes replied.

Erin and Drew smiled at her. Erin was extremely beautiful. She was average height with a curvy figure. She wore her hair in this long goddess braid that made her look almost angelic. Drew was equally attractive with a banging ass body that made Lourdes' shape look average. Drew was rocking her hair in faux locks with half of them pulled up away from her face.

Both of the women were giving Lourdes nothing but good vibes.

"Well somehow me and my sisters all married brothers," Erin said and laughed while touching her small baby bump.

Lourdes laughed with them. "That seems cool, though. You all are family and stuff. How many months are you?"

"Five," Erin replied.

"Yeah we're all fertile as hell too," Drew said making them all laugh.

"Hell yeah, we are. You have to come hang with us in the D. Do you have kids?" Erin asked her.

Lourdes shook her head at the same time Qwote happened to look at her. He was talking with Aamil, but also keeping his eye on his woman. He couldn't help but to see how sad she looked when hit with the questions of kids and marriage. He made note of it and went back to his conversation.

"Nope. I just moved back to Detroit. I was in school in New York. I would love to hook back up with y'all in Detroit, though. You two seem cool, and I know my girl Sundae would love to hang as well," she said.

Erin and Drew smiled. "Definitely, then let's link up," Drew told her.

"Aye y'all ready to hit up the club?" Kasam asked walking up to all of them.

Qwote made his way over to Lourdes, and he wrapped his arms around her small waist as he hugged her from the back.

Lourdes looked at Kasam up close and got lost in his hazel eyes. He wiped the sweat away from his forehead as he looked at her.

Damn he fine as fuck, shit him and his brother, she thought smiling at him. Qwote tightened his hold on her and Kasam looked at him. A smile spread across his face.

"What up, nigga! I see you made it," he said.

Qwote chuckled. "Hell yeah! That show was good as hell. Kasam, this is my girl Lourdes," He said introducing the two.

Lourdes smiled at Kasam shyly and Erin laughed. "Don't smile at my baby too damn hard," she joked making them all laugh.

Lourdes looked away and Erin smiled warmly at her. "I'm just playing, girl. Everybody is like that when they first meet his crazy ass," she said not wanting Lourdes to be embarrassed.

Lourdes nodded. She wasn't trying to be a groupie; she had simply had a fan girl moment, because for years she had listened to him on the radio. However, she felt Erin was being nice, so she didn't feel uncomfortable.

"Yeah please forgive my wife. She goes crazy over a nigga. You see she pregnant right now trying to keep me locked down and shit," Kasam said grabbing Erin up and kissed her all over her neck.

Erin laughed and pushed him away only for him to grab her up again.

"Lourdes, don't listen to him. I can't go to the fucking bathroom without him calling to see where I'm at," she said and all of the women laughed.

Lourdes watched as Kasam and Erin kissed each other. She could see the love that Erin and Drew shared with their men. She saw that they all had something in common. They were all crazy in love and lucky to be with the men that held the keys to their heart. Only she once again felt left out, because her and Qwote were the only couple that wasn't married with a kid. Lourdes tucked in her pain from not sharing that with them and found the strength to go to the club and have fun. After partying at LIV until the wee hours of the morning, Qwote took Lourdes back to the beach. Lourdes was a little fucked up, so Qwote held her heels in one hand as they walked along the shoreline.

"Did you have fun tonight?" he asked her.

Lourdes nodded while smiling. "Yeah I really did. I like Drew and Erin," she said.

"That's what's up. They seem cool. I see they all married and shit," he said making her look at him.

"Yeah they are," she said.

Qwote nodded. "You know I still remember the first time I seen you. You were bringing me my dog back that had run away from us, and me and Quamir was arguing over who was going to talk to you. Of course, I won but that nigga still tried it. Man, when I saw we were all going to the same high school I was so fucking geeked. I know we had a lot of problems back then, but we still stayed together. Then you left for college, and I was happy for you, but I was also mad for a little while. I didn't have my rock with me. A nigga felt empty out here," he said and looked away from her for a moment. The only thing that you could hear was the water hitting the shore.

"But I got my shit together. I took my classes and started my company. I always told myself I had to make it for us. You have always been a *priority* for me, Lourdes. When I was shopping for your ring the other day, I kept asking myself what kind of ring would even be good enough for the woman that you love? I mean you're priceless to me, bae, but I think I did you some justice."

Qwote stopped walking and he looked at Lourdes. She stared up at him in shock. She couldn't believe what was happening. Qwote went into his pocket and pulled out a small ring box. He opened it and Lourdes looked at the ring. It was dark, but she could still see the silhouette of the ring. Her eyes instantly watered.

"I'ma keep it simple, baby. I love you, and I wanna spend infinity with your ass. Will you marry me?" he asked.

Lourdes slowly nodded and he placed the ring on her finger. He put the box away and picked her up. Lourdes cried as he kissed her passionately on the lips. "I love you, baby," she whispered against his lips.

Qwote pulled back from the kiss to look up at her. "I love you too, *Mi Amor*."

A few days after Lourdes went home, she and Qwote attended Sundae's birthday party that was being thrown in Downtown Detroit at V nightclub inside of the MGM Grand Casino hotel. Qwote chilled by the bar while Lourdes sat with Sundae. Sundae couldn't get over how beautiful and elegant Lourdes' oval shaped, Tacori, diamond engagement ring was. It was simply stunning and Lourdes, of course, loved it as well.

"I'm so happy for you. Now you can ease up on your man some. Damn this nigga loves you, and you know that shit, Lourdes," she said and they both smiled.

"I know. I know. I was tripping but hell we done been together for years. I think as women we sometimes do so much to please others that we forget to please ourselves. I woke up one day and was tired of fronting like I was cool with not being his wife. I do everything to make him happy, so I'm happy to see that he's willing to do the same for me. What's up with you, though? This your fifth shot, ain't you breastfeeding?" Lourdes asked Sundae.

Sundae tossed the Patron back and gave Lourdes a big smile. She was two weeks into no Quamir and *damn* it had been hard. He had been hounding her at her job, and at the moment was across the room glaring at her like she wasn't there with her husband. Sundae was only trying to do the right thing, but she felt so empty inside because what felt right to her was being with Quamir. She knew her family deserved a shot at being whole. So there she was miserable at her own birthday party, and praying the men she loved didn't tear the club up. Sundae took a deep breath and exhaled.

"I'm going through some shit that needs to be in a book," Sundae said no longer being able to hide the pain she was feeling.

Lourdes touched her arm. "What's wrong?"

Sundae went to reply and stopped. In some black jeans with a distressed grey, Yeezy sweater, Quamir swaggered his way over to them holding a bag. Sundae suddenly became nervous, and her eyes instantly shifted to see where Drama was at. She frantically tried to locate him as Quamir walked up on them. He gave Lourdes a quick hug then walked over to Sundae.

"Stand up," he told her more than a little tipsy.

Sundae shook her head. "Quamir...you need to leave," she said looking up at him.

Lourdes watched the scene unfold while shaking her head.

"Leave? Why the fuck would I do that? Stand up so I can give you your gift, baby," he said.

Lourdes stood up and waved Qwote over. She then walked up on Quamir and grabbed his arm.

"Please don't do this, Quamir. You have Darby now. Don't cause drama just because."

Quamir shot Lourdes a glare before snatching his arm away from her. "Fuck Darby! That ain't my bitch," He looked back at Sundae and licked his lips. "Baby, why you tripping?"

"Nigga, why the fuck you over here?" Drama asked walking up with some guys he knew.

Quamir chuckled as he looked his way. He smirked at Drama, and Drama punched him in the face so hard he fell back over a chair and landed on his back. All of the attention immediately went to them. Drama ran up on Quamir and kicked him in the face. Qwote moved fast to shove Drama out of the way and went to him when Lourdes grabbed his arm.

"Qwote, no! Let's go!" she yelled.

Quamir slowly stood up a little dazed by the punch. He grabbed Sundae's birthday bag that had fallen on the floor as Frenchie ran over to them. Drama and his boys stood across from Quamir, and his people and Sundae sat in her seat in complete shock at what had happened. She slowly stood up and walked up on Drama. She grabbed his arm, and he looked down at her angrily ready to finish fucking Quamir up. He'd watched him stare at Sundae all night, and he told himself the minute he stepped out of line he was going to pop his ass.

"Baby, let's go," she said looking up at him.

Drama shook his head. He wanted to do everything but leave. One of the men Drama was chilling with was Kasam. Drama was working on Kasam's new CD, and also working with some of Kasam's artist. Kasam walked up on him and whispered something in his ear before looking at Qwote who he was also cool with.

"Man, y'all better than this. Let's go before they call the cops on our black asses. I don't know about y'all, but I'm not trying to go to jail. You bound to die in the fucking cop car en route to the fucking station and shit nowadays," he said dead ass serious.

Qwote stared at Kasam for a moment before going over to Quamir and pulling him away. Lourdes shot Sundae an apologetic smile before following after her man, his brother, and friends. Sundae looked up at Drama and his eyes stared straight ahead. She followed his gaze and saw that he was staring at the birthday bag that Quamir had for her that sat on a nearby table. Drama shook his head trying to calm himself down.

"When I see that nigga again it's over for his ass, Sundae," he said and walked away. Sundae held onto his arm and quietly walked with him out of the packed club.

Chapter Eighteen

"Look I need you to handle that shit now! I also need for you to stab me," Darby said pacing back and forth. She'd just found out through social media that Lourdes and Qwote were engaged. She was so enraged she didn't know what to do.

Tevin looked up at her and blew a thick cloud of kush smoke out of his mouth. He thought that he knew what crazy was until he met Darby. She was a straight up head case. One minute she was cool, the next she was off onto some other shit. He slipped her Percocet's sometimes, and she would really be a cool chick, but on most day she was on one.

"Look why the fuck would I stab you?" He asked sitting up and resting his elbows onto his knees.

Darby looked at him and dramatically fell to the ground. Tevin and a few other hustlers that were around chuckled. She was so fucking extra at times. "Because I need you to. I'm willing to give you ten thousand dollars, Tevin," she replied as she looked up sadly.

Darby felt like her life was over. She didn't know what to do. Qwote had somehow fell under Lourdes' trap and was now engaged to her. Darby was driving herself crazy as she thought of ways to tear them apart. She decided to not get Sundae attacked but to instead have Lourdes fucked up maybe even killed. Shit she was at the point where she no longer cared what happened as long as Lourdes was out of her way.

"Ma, I'm all for some easy money. I just know how you get down. You got that bad ass bitch Palma that I used to fuck in trouble playing this game with you. I ain't the one, I'd be done killed your ass for fucking me over."

Darby looked up at him. "Palma was already on the run. She got all types of warrants, so don't listen to what that bitch gotta say about me. She and I was never friends we only worked together. I would never do that to you. Shit, I need you too bad to do that," she said truthfully.

Tevin laughed as he stood up. He walked up on Darby and helped her stand. "Aye, y'all look out for them boys. I need to talk to my pretty little crazy girl for a moment," he said and pulled her to the back of the house. Tevin took her into a room and closed the door. He checked the window to make sure all was good before he turned his attention back to Darby. For some reason, he felt for her. She was crazy but hell so was he. She had some good pussy and she was pretty. However, he didn't like the path she was going down.

"Ma, why the fuck you so obsessed with these people? A few months ago you were so cool. You would come through the block, chill with a nigga, and do your thang. Now, you always on some revenge type shit. You gon' fuck around and let this bullshit drive you crazy," he warned her.

Darby walked around the room in a circle until she stood still and stared down at the floor. She was worried that she was going to completely lose Qwote. She loved him and she wanted him for herself. If she couldn't have him she refused to let Lourdes have him.

"I can't let her have him. She just doesn't deserve him," Darby said quietly.

Tevin walked up behind her and kissed her neck. He touched her hips and slid his hand around to her stomach. "Is this my baby?" he asked her.

Darby shrugged and they both smiled. "Yo ass ain't shit. You know you not doing that man right anyway, Darby. I'm saying let this shit go. Fuck them," he said sliding her jeans down her legs.

Darby shook her head as if his suggestion was ludicrous. "I can't do that. I love him," she said.

Tevin pushed Darby onto the bed and pulled his pants down. He didn't have time to get naked and really what was the point? They weren't at a room, they were at the spot.

"Yeah and I love my girl but look at us. Now open them legs up you been keeping this away from me way too long," He said and climbed between her thighs.

Darby smiled and willingly spread her legs. Tevin slid in and slowly penetrated her. She closed her eyes and imagined it was Qwote.

After spending another hour at the spot, Darby left to grab some tums and go home. She walked into the pharmacy by her home and spotted Lourdes arguing with Frenchie on the next aisle. Darby smiled as she pulled out her cellphone to record what was happening.

"Look this is crazy. You can't be fucking following me, Frenchie. What the fuck is wrong with you?" She could hear Lourdes ask him.

"I'm trying to say congrats and see if you would come to see my moms with me. She's fucking dying, Lourdes. This is all I ever asked you to fucking do, and you play me like this?" he asked through gritted teeth.

Darby was so excited by her luck she could have cried as she continued to record their conversation.

"Look…. I'm sorry about your mom. You know I love her. After this, though, you have to leave me alone, or I will tell Qwote and I'm not playing. So when do you wanna go?"

"I can pick you up tomorrow at noon and we can go. How is that?" he asked.

"It's cool. Look, I gotta go," she could hear Lourdes say.

Darby ended the recording and stuck her face into a magazine for a few minutes as she waited for them to empty out of the next aisle. Darby then grabbed her Tums and got herself a bottle of wine. Fuck some heartburn she was back on track to getting her man. That alone called for a huge celebration.

****

The next day Lourdes awoke with Qwote sliding in and out of her. She closed her eyes and moaned while enjoying the pleasure.

"Mmmm...Qwote."

Qwote pulled her head back so that he could suck on the side of her neck. Lourdes squeezed down hard onto him making him groan. His hand gripped her hip tightly as he fucked her harder while they lay on their sides.

"Throw it back," he said in a low voice.

Lourdes moaned and started throwing it back at him. Qwote slid his hand around to the front of her and started to slowly rub her clitoris. Lourdes whimpered as her pussy contracted against his dick.

"Baby...damn...shit," she moaned.

Qwote rubbed harder until she erupted all over him. He then pushed her off of her side and onto her stomach. He pulled her onto her knees and slid all the way inside of her. Qwote pumped fluidly in and out of her. All that could be heard through the room were sounds of their lovemaking. Lourdes was so wet Qwote got lost in the feeling and ended up coming inside of her. They both collapsed onto the bed and Qwote looked over at Lourdes.

"Morning, bae," he said and gave her a lazy smile.

Lourdes licked her lips and smiled at him. "Morning."

"So what's the plan for today?" he said sitting up.

Lourdes stared at his beautifully sculpted body for a moment. "Nothing just running errands. What about you?" she asked.

Qwote looked down at her for a moment. He loved Lourdes so much so that he was adjusting his plans in life for her. He wanted her to be fully satisfied with him, and the relationship that they had. He didn't regret for a minute proposing to her.

"Shit. I got a meeting with this new client at eleven thirty then I'ma hit up the gym with Quamir. That nigga has been walking around like somebody killed his fucking dog and shit since Sundae's party. I'm still pissed that shit happened."

Lourdes shook her. She too was in shock by what had transpired at the party. Since then Quamir seemed to shut down. He wasn't going to work and had been physically sick. Sundae was calling Lourdes daily to check on him, and Lourdes was tired of telling her friend to just leave it alone. Lourdes felt like Sundae and Quamir were wrong for whatever they had going on.

"Yeah please do that, and I'll see you tonight."

Qwote looked at Lourdes' sweaty, naked body and smiled.

"Yeah you will. I'ma need for you to get on some birth control, baby, cause a nigga tired of pulling out, and also pick up that morning after pill. Just because we're doing the wedding doesn't mean we gotta rush the baby shit," he said. He stood up to not have to see the look on Lourdes' face that he knew she had at the mention of the morning after pill.

"Okay," she replied with an eye roll.

Qwote ignored the tone of her voice and walked out of the room. They were newly engaged. Lourdes could only demand so much from him. He wasn't about to go against everything that he believed in just because she was pouting about it.

196

Qwote took a quick shower and slipped into one of his signature custom-made suits before leaving the condo. Lourdes moved around a little slower than he did. She took her time washing up then she made coffee and straightened up while it brewed. She played Khelani's new CD and listened to her soulful voice fill the condo's rooms while she wondered how the day would go.

She was lying to Qwote and going to visit Frenchie's mother. When Lourdes met Qwote he immediately brought her around his family and friends. Back then they were all kids. She took to them all and loved Frenchie's mother. She felt extremely bad that his mom had a brain tumor. She also felt like Frenchie was using it as an opportunity to be alone with her.

When he'd visited her a year prior in New York she thought nothing of it. She was excited to see a familiar face and had even invited him over to her place for drinks, and so that they could catch up. Things happened that really shouldn't have and Lourdes was beginning to second guess herself. She threw on some clothes not trying to be even remotely appealing to Frenchie and she called him on her cell.

"Aye, I was headed your way," he said picking up.

His tone was so light and jovial. Lourdes knew she was about to upset him, but she really didn't care. This was about his mother, yet she also needed to feel comfortable with the situation. Riding in an enclosed space with him was not comforting to her.

"Hey about that. I have something to do later so I will just drive. Text me her address."

"Lolo," Frenchie said through gritted teeth. Lourdes sighed grabbing her bag.

"Should we discuss what happened the last time you were in a small space with me?" she asked.

Frenchie sighed. "I'm sending it now," he said and ended the call.

Lourdes grabbed her stuff and walked out of the room. She bent the corner and bumped right into Qwote. She grabbed her chest completely caught off guard by his presence, and he smiled at her. He pecked her lips and gave her a once over. Lourdes was dressed comfortably in boyfriend jeans with a white cami, a black cardigan, and light weight jacket on top of the outfit. She wore her ballet flats with no makeup or jewelry besides her engagement ring.

"Hey, ma, you looking good. I forgot my work cell here," he said as Lourdes' phone started to ring.

Lourdes heart nearly jumped from out of her chest. She wasn't for sure but she could just feel that it was Frenchie calling her back. Qwote noticed how off she was acting and he frowned. He'd blew back a midday blunt after his meeting to clear his head, so he wasn't sure if he was bugging or if it was her.

"You good, bae?"

Lourdes nodded and kissed him again. Qwote pulled her bottom lip into his mouth, and he backed her against the wall as Frenchie called her yet again. Lourdes got lost in the kiss as she silenced the call. Qwote's hands found her ass and they squeezed down hard on it. Qwote started to kiss on her neck as he unbuttoned her jeans.

"Just let me suck on that pretty pussy until you cum, and I promise I'll let you go," he said sliding her jeans down.

Lourdes forced herself to grab the jeans and pull them back up. She looked at Qwote and knew he was pissed. He didn't like the word no because he rarely heard it.

"Bae, I have to go. I promise I got you tonight," she said buttoning her jeans back up.

Qwote took a step back and stroked his beard. "You go get that pill today?"

Shit! Lourdes thought. She had been cleaning and was so worked up on Frenchie that she forgot all about the pill.

"Yeah I did," she lied.

Qwote stared in her eyes for a moment and nodded. He leaned towards her and grabbed her face. He squeezed her cheeks a little hard as he stared down at her. "You better be butt naked with some red bottoms on and a wet pussy when I come up in here tonight. You hear me?"

"Yes, baby," Lourdes replied looking up at him.

Qwote leaned down and slowly slide his tongue into her mouth. Lourdes caressed it for several minutes before she pulled back. She gave Qwote one last look before stepping away and leaving out of the condo. Lourdes got the address to where Frenchie's mother was at and put it in her GPS. As

Lourdes pulled up into the parking lot, she prayed that she wasn't doing anything that could tear apart what she had with her man.

"I'm just visiting his sick mother. Qwote can't fault me for that," she said and exited the car.

A few seconds later Frenchie pulled up in his Mercedes and parked behind her car. Lourdes stood nervously as he exited his car looking like a model in his black jeans with his black Polo on with a black bomber jacket to match. Frenchie licked his full lips as he walked up on Lourdes. He gave her a slight hug and stepped back.

"You smell like him," he said as they walked off.

Lourdes glanced over at him. "Like who? My fiancé?"

Frenchie grabbed her and grinned at her. "Yeah. You smell just like that nigga," he said and took her into the building.

Lourdes ignored his reply, and she walked with him into the building. She was eventually able to get her hand out of his grip. They signed in at the front desk and were quickly taken back to his mother's room. Frenchie allowed for Lourdes to walk in first and what Lourdes saw broke her heart. Frenchie's mother was a gorgeous woman, but her illness had taken a toll on her body. She was incredibly thin with a bandaged head. Lourdes eyes watered as she walked over to the bed.

"Is that Lolo?"

Lolo was Lourde's nickname when she was younger that Qwote had given her. Since then he had upgraded her to *Mi Amor* but that name was exclusively for him. Frenchie knew that Qwote would go apeshit on him for calling her that, so he simply called her Lolo or Lourdes.

"Hey, Miss Marie, it is. How are you?" Lourdes asked walking over to the bed to sit in the chair that was closest to it.

Marie's chestnut colored eyes landed on Lourdes and a small smile spread across her face. She held her small frail hand out and Lourdes took it as she sat down. Frenchie stood near the wall with his eyes on the ceiling. He'd let on to his mother for years about how he was secretly in love with Lourdes. Marie felt like maybe she could try before she left the earth to set her son up with someone that he genuinely loved, and that she knew would look after him for her.

"I missed you, girl. You forgot about little old me," Marie joked and coughed a little.

Lourdes smiled and handed her a small cup of water. Marie drunk it down and gave Lourdes the cup back.

"Of course not, Marie. I've always loved you. I remember you used to have the best homemade cookies and cakes around. You the one that taught me all of those recipes."

Marie smiled remembering the good times. "Yeah you were the only girl that constantly hung out with them boys. Hell, I had to teach it to somebody, and your friend Sundae told me she didn't like cooking, so I left her alone," Marie said making them both laugh.

Marie's eyes went to Frenchie's and she cleared her throat. "Frenchie, can you give us a minute, son? I need to speak with Lourdes alone," she announced.

Frenchie nodded and stepped out of the room. The door closed and Marie looked at Lourdes.

"I'm sick. I'm sure you can see that. Frenchie didn't lure you here, I really wanted to see you. Yesterday all of my boys came to see me including Qwote. He's grown to be so handsome too. Until this day he still talks about you with nothing but love." Marie stopped talking to lick her dry lips. "My son has been in love with you since the moment Qwote brought you to the neighborhood. I love him too much to break his heart, but I just had to tell him eventually that you were already taken, so I'm not calling you here for that. I actually want you to just look after him. His brother is dead, Lourdes. His father never cared about him, and his sister is going to be too busy grieving over me to worry about Fred. I love those kids and I hate it, but it's almost my time to go. Can you promise to just make sure he's okay? Please, Lourdes, make sure his boys stay rallied around him so that he can get through this. I have maybe a month left if that. I'm holding on but I can feel it. My God is calling me home, baby, and I'm ready to go," she said with a peaceful look on her face.

Lourdes wiped her tears while nodding. Marie grabbed her hand and smiled at her.

"Sweetie, I'm okay. I'm ready. I'm tired, and I've been battling this thing for a very long time. I'm just worried about my son and daughter. Now my baby girl has her husband, but Frenchie only has those boys and you. I know about New York, and I told him off about that, but he has a good heart. He would never do any harm to you, Lourdes. He loves you too much for that. So can you promise me you will make sure he's good?" Marie asked.

Lourdes nodded. "Yes, I promise."

Marie searched Lourdes' face for a moment before smiling. She sighed and squeezed Lourdes hand.

"Now tell me about how you have been," she said smiling at Lourdes.

Lourdes relaxed in the seat and began to go over the past few years of her life with Marie.

Chapter Nineteen

"I'ma need for you to tell me what the fuck is going on with you and Quamir," Lourdes said to Sundae.

Sundae rocked her baby as she sat down across from Lourdes. She planted her eyes on her beautiful best friend and she shrugged. "I was confused but I'm good now. Just know that I cut him off way before my party."

Lourdes looked at Sundae and slowly shook her head. Sundae and Lourdes were inside of the Cheesecake Factory catching up. It had been a week since Lourdes saw Marie, and she had been sneaking away to help Frenchie clean out Marie's house.

"Sundae, really. Why would you do that?" Sundae shrugged. She looked down at her beautiful baby girl and felt beyond sad. There wasn't any way to really explain it other than being brutally honest.

"I fucked up. I miss him. When I was away with you in New York I could deal with it, but now that I'm back home I feel it. Drama does too. He knows that our chemistry isn't the same, but he's trying not to acknowledge it. I love Quamir. I always will Lourdes and I feel…." Sundae cleared her throat and held back her tears. "I feel so empty inside. I'm living a life with another man that I should be living with him. I'm going to put my daughter first and live with the mistakes that

I have made, but damn it still doesn't make the shit easier to deal with," she replied.

Lourdes sipped some of her water and looked away from Sundae for a moment. She wasn't sure what she could say. Hell, she felt for her but the reality was Sundae was now married to Drama, and that's who Lourdes felt she should stay with, still she felt for her friend. She could hear the pain in Sundae's voice and that was breaking Lourdes' heart.

"I'm sorry you're going through this, Sundae. To me, you have it all. I know Drama isn't Quamir, but maybe you can learn to love him the same. Stop comparing the two and start to love Drama. Get to really know him and love him as the man he is."

"I could try. I mean I have but I can again. I'm not ready to give up on my family, Lourdes. I just… miss him."

"Did you two fuck?" Lourdes asked quietly.

Sundae blushed and put her head down. Lourdes kicked her leg under the table.

"Your little hot pussy ass. How could you? Sundae, damn," Lourdes said while shaking her head.

"I know. I know, and I swear it only happened once. I even took the morning after pill," Sundae lied and Lourdes sat upright with wide eyes.

"Sundae. Shit!" Lourdes said remembering she forgot to get the pill.

"What?"

Lourdes scratched her head while laughing nervously. She was really fucking up. "So I guess it's my confession time now. Not only have I been seeing Frenchie behind Qwote's back to help him prepare for Marie's death, I also forgot to get the morning after pill when I told Qwote that I did already. What the fuck am I going to do if I'm pregnant?" she asked.

"Well let's talk about the pill first. You probably aren't pregnant off that one time if that was y'all only slip up, so I wouldn't even stress that. Now onto Frenchie. Bitch, how you gonna go in on me when you fucking with him?"

Lourdes looked at Sundae and rolled her eyes before laughing. "I'm not fucking with him. Marie asked me to watch over him, and that's what I'm trying to do."

Sundae shook her head. Lourdes was always trying to save someone.

"That's not your job to do that shit. Qwote gon' kill both of y'all asses if he finds this shit out. I mean you're happy with your man, why do you keep finding ways to fuck up what y'all got? And after that New York shit, you shouldn't even wanna fuck with Frenchie like that," Sundae said.

Lourdes sighed. "I know but you didn't see what I did. Marie pulled at my heart strings, Sundae. I couldn't say no to her," she said.

Sundae nodded with pursed lips. "So you put Frenchie and Marie's feelings over Qwote's because that's what it comes down to. Marie is trying to look out for her son. She could give a damn about Qwote but you should. That is your man, right?"

Lourdes glared at her friend. "Bitch, stop talking and pass me my baby," she said and they both laughed.

Sundae passed Lourdes the baby, and they continued to talk before parting ways. Sundae then went home and smiled when she saw Drama's truck in her circular driveway.

"Your daddy's home little girl," she said parking.

Sundae quickly grabbed Zoe and walked up to the house. Drama opened the door before she could unlock it. He was wearing a black beater with basketball shorts and Jordan flip flops. Sundae smiled at him and he grabbed their daughter.

"Hey, babe, I thought you had to go to the Chi," she said following him into the house.

"Nah, I changed my mind," he said.

"Hey, daddy's girl. What you doing?" he asked carrying Zoe down their long hallway and into the family room.

Sundae took off her shoes and joined them on the couch. She looked around and smiled at how clean everything was.

"You cleaned up too?"

Drama chuckled. "Hell nah. I had the cleaning service come today. I got Chef George in there cooking now."

Sundae's eyes lit up. "Really? I thought I smelled something. Well let me go freshen up and we can eat. Do you want me to get the baby?"

Drama shook his head while looking at her. His intense gaze was making her uneasy.

"Nah, you good. Go do you," he said.

Sundae frowned at him. "What you mean go do me?"

Drama looked at her like she was crazy and looked back at his baby girl. "Momma over here tripping," he said and Zoe's hazel eyes looked at him.

Sundae laughed nervously and stood up. "Yeah I am. I'll be back," she said and quickly walked away.

Sundae went up to their bedroom and stripped out of her clothes. She thought about what Lourdes said as she turned her shower on. Drama was fine. He wasn't lacking in the looks department. He had a big dick, he was a good man, and he was a good provider, plus he was great with Zoe. Okay, he worked a lot but she would rather he worked a lot over him not having a job at all.

"Yeah I love Quamir but Drama is cool too. I have to let him go and do right by my family," she said and walked over to the mirror.

Sundae looked at herself and was happy to see her body was back to pre-pregnancy weight. Her skin was still glowing. Her breast hadn't appeared to drop any from breastfeeding, like so many women had said that they would. Her hips were wider and she had a little bit more fat in her face giving her chunky cheeks but she liked it. Sundae had been many things, but insecure had never been one of them. She welcomed the changes her body had made to bring a life into the world.

After taking a long hot shower, Sundae got out and dried off. She put her wet hair into a hair tie and put on a silk robe.

Sundae walked into her bedroom and Drama sat at the foot of their large bed with his eyes glued to the plasma TV that was mounted on the wall facing the bed. Sundae didn't have to look at the screen to know what he was watching because she could hear it.

"Nah you gon' take this dick, baby. This still my shit ain't it?" he asked.

"Yes… damn yes," Sundae could hear herself respond.

Sundae closed her eyes as she could feel the heat from Drama's gaze land on her. She slowly tried to back up, but he was on her so fast she didn't have a chance to. Drama grabbed Sundae by her ponytail and pulled her out of the room. Sundae eventually fell and Drama began to drag her out of the bedroom wearing only her robe.

"Draven, please!" she yelled terrified as to what he was about to do to her.

"Shut your ass up,' Drama hissed at her.

He snatched her up off of the floor and tossed her over his shoulder. He took the stairs two at a time and walked into the kitchen. The chef, who was also his first cousin, was very confused as to what was going on as Drama walked in on him cooking.

"Aye, I gotta make a run. I need for you to watch Zoe. She's asleep in the family room in the bassinet. It won't take long," he said and walked off.

Drama went to the garage and threw Sundae into the passenger seat of his car, making her hit her head on the window. Sundae cried harder as he got into the car and checked the middle console for his gun. Sundae watched him check the chamber and her eyes grew wide. Too scared to even speak, she watched him as he backed out of the garage then out of the driveway. Drama was so angry his hand shook against the steering wheel as he drove.

"I'ma give you one chance to make this shit right. If you don't I promise you I'ma kill that nigga," he said quietly.

"Draven, I'm so sorry. I didn't..." Sundae said in a shaky voice.

"Shut the fuck up talking to me, Sundae, before I knock you in your shit," Drama said cutting her off.

Sundae swallowed hard and put her seat belt on. She was wearing a silk robe with nothing else on while Drama drove his car fast to Quamir's house. The closer he got the more worried Sundae became. She had never seen Drama even get angry before. She expected him to maybe hit her, at the worst, then leave, but he had some other shit in mind. Drama tossed his cellphone in Sundae's lap and glared over at her.

"Call that nigga and put it on speaker," he demanded as they pulled into Quamir's driveway.

Sundae called Quamir with a shaky hand and put the call on speaker. She wanted to ask Drama how he even knew where Quamir lived, but she knew better than to do that.

"Aye, Drama, you get my tape?" Quamir asked smugly as he answered the phone.

Sundae's heart did a flip flop at the sound of his voice.

211

"Nigga, I got that tape. Why don't you bring you bitter ass outside?" Drama said and ended the call. He put his phone away and he grabbed his gun. He took the safety off and Sundae looked at him.

"Draven, don't do this," Sundae pleaded with him.

Drama shot her a look. "Don't say shit else to me. I'm two second away from knocking all the teeth out of your motherfucking mouth, bitch," he said.

Sundae sat back taking heed to his warning. Quamir emerged from the house after a few minutes in workout gear. He had on gray sweats with a gray, long sleeved Nike muscle shirt that showed off every muscle in his arm and his abs. Drama sucked his teeth and grabbed his gun as he emerged from the car. Sundae opened the car door and Quamir's eyes fell onto her. He looked at her then at Drama. A slick ass grin slid across his handsome face.

"Nigga, what is this?" he asked highly amused at the scene before him.

"Nigga, this ain't shit to laugh about. Sundae, get yo ass over here!" Drama yelled.

Sundae rushed over to him and he grabbed her face. He looked down at her and she saw nothing but pain in his eyes. What was crazy was it was the same pain that she saw in Quamir's eyes when she hurt him. Sundae felt so bad behind what she had done, but Drama was handling the situation all wrong.

"I'm sorry, baby."

"No, she not! You didn't hear how she was loving the dick. Tossing that wet ass pussy all over a nigga's dick. I hope you know I shot off all inside of that shit too. She probably pregnant with my baby right now," Quamir bragged.

Sundae grabbed Drama's face to keep him looking at her.

"I'm sorry. I wanna be with you. I'm so sorry, baby. I'm so sorry. I love you," she cried. Drama shook his head.

"Tell that nigga," he demanded.

Sundae looked at Quamir, the man she loved. The man she was still, after all those years, in love with, and she shook her head. He'd set her up and foolishly she'd taken the bait. She opened her mouth to speak to him and a gun went off.

POP!

Chapter Twenty

"You gotta stop this, Darby. I had a dream that somebody tried to kill you. You know all my dreams come to life," Kirk said walking around Darby's living room.

Darby smiled at him as she ate her cereal. She was doing good. She'd been working double time to take Qwote away from Lourdes, now she was simply waiting for the fall out to happen, because she knew it would.

"Kirk, I've been good. I haven't gotten high all week. I stopped fucking most of my clients. I only do the big spenders now since I'm showing, and I've been leaving people alone. Why are you here?" she asked and giggled.

Kirk looked at Darby with his head cocked to the side. She was happy, so yeah he knew she had done some fucked up shit or was planning on doing some fucked up shit.

"Darby, I know you think those dreams be games but the shit is real," he said as someone knocked on the door.

Darby stood up laughing. She walked over to the door and pulled it open. She saw no one so she turned to Kirk.

"I'm good, Kirk. I promise you I am," she assured him as Palma walked up behind her.

Palma pushed Darby into the house and shut the door. Kirk looked at Palma and then at Darby. He shook his head. Palma held onto a sharp-edged hunting knife.

"Palma, what's up beautiful? I haven't seen you in a while," He said smiling calmly at her.

Kirk nor Darby were strangers to someone pulling a weapon out on them. Kirk was happy to be with the Lord, but he was upset that he had been caught slipping. Since he had been in church, he had stopped carrying his gun on him.

"Fuck you, Kirk and, bitch, I'ma kill you! Why the fuck would you give them my info. The fucking police are after me for some shit you did!" Palma yelled and sliced the knife into Darby's cheek. The blade was so sharp Darby didn't even feel the cut, but she felt the blood drip down her cheek.

"Bitch, you cut me!" She yelled and punched Palma in the face.

Palma tried to cut her again as Kirk ran over to them. He jumped in front of Darby and Palma ended up stabbing him in the stomach. He pushed her back before he fell down. Darby looked at him then at Palma, who was back on her feet. Darby ran to the back of her condo as fast as she could trying to get to her gun. She tried to bend the corner and she felt the knife go into her back.

"Bitch, I'ma backstab you the same way you did me," Palma said and ran out of the condo as Darby fell to the ground and landed on her stomach.

Chapter Twenty-One

"Hi, Miss Lourdes, we need a check," Juno said.

Lourdes pulled up to her condo and parked behind Qwote's Audi. She watched as some woman with a hat on and dark shades exited Darby's front door in a hurry. Lourdes frowned wondering who she was before going back to the call.

"Juno, a check for what? Didn't Qwote pay you?" she asked.

"In the past yeah. He told me today that he wasn't to be contacted again about the house, and to take the prices up with you. I need another $10,000 to keep working, and I'll need more money in two weeks. We're so close to being done. I would hate to have to stop."

Lourdes sighed not sure what was going on. "Juno, please continue on the house. I'll bring the check for you in the morning. Okay?"

Juno chuckled. "Yes. Yes. Good, I'll see you then, Miss Lourdes," he said and hung up the phone.

Lourdes grabbed her bag and exited the car. She walked up to her front door and went to unlock it when she saw it was opened. She pushed the door in and spotted boxes all over her condo. Lourdes quickly went in and saw that most of the stuff was packed up.

"Qwote! Qwote! Qwote!"

"Yeah," he said walking out of the kitchen with a box.

Lourdes looked at him. He wore dark jeans with an HBA hoodie on and black Timbs. He had his fitted on so low she could barely see his eyes. Lourdes wasn't sure what was going on, but she knew he was pissed.

"Qwote, what are you doing?"

Qwote ignored her and put the box down by the door. He walked back by her and she grabbed his arm. He jerked his arm away so hard she stumbled back.

"Don't fucking touch me. Go touch that nigga Frenchie," he said angrily.

"Frenchie! Qwote, wait a minute and just talk to me," Lourdes said going behind him.

Lourdes followed Qwote into the back on the condo and saw that he had packed up all of his clothes from the bedroom. She started to cry as he threw his jewelry into his leather backpack.

"You mad because I went with him to see his dying mother?" she asked incredulously.

Qwote stopped packing to look at her. "Nah, I'm mad that you continuously lied to my fucking face. I gave you chance after chance to tell me what you were fucking doing. Save them motherfucking tears for that nigga. What I need for you to do is get the fuck out of me face," he snapped and went back to packing.

Lourdes wiped her eyes. "So I'm the bad guy for helping your friend out? Wow, okay," she said.

Qwote dropped his diamond bedazzled watch onto the bed and walked up on Lourdes. He grabbed her cheeks and squeezed down as hard as he could while making her look up at him.

"No, you wrong for chilling with that nigga in New York and never mentioning that shit to me. You wrong for sitting up under that nigga all fucking week like you his bitch. That's what the fuck you wrong about. Stop fucking playing with me," he said and let her go.

Qwote had never spoken to Lourdes that way before. Lourdes fell down to the ground and pulled her knees to her chest. She honestly didn't know what to say. She hadn't done anything wrong.

"I love you, and I would never cheat on you. I was just helping your friend."

Qwote continued to pack his stuff up ignoring her.

"Qwote, please. I...I forgot to get the morning after pill. I could be pregnant," she said reaching. At the moment, she would have said anything to keep him.

Qwote chuckled. "Of course, you did. You already tricked me into proposing to you now you trying to trap me with a baby? Bitch, you out of your mind. I should have never came back to yo ass," he said and grabbed the last of his things. He walked to the door and scratched his chin.

"I'ma need that ring back, and if you are pregnant do the right thing because I don't want yo ass," he said holding his hand out. "And a baby won't get me back," he said angrily.

Lourdes bottom lip shook as she silently cried. She took off the ring and threw it at Qwote. He found it on the floor and picked it up.

"You be good. Now you free to hop on Frenchie's dick and fuck with a few bitches too while you at it," he said and walked away.

Lourdes fell onto the floor and cried the ugliest cry that she had ever cried. She cried until her tears clouded her vision and her nose leaked. She wiped the snot with the back of her hand and shook her head. She couldn't believe Qwote had left her. All she did was help Frenchie prepare for his mother's death, and Qwote used that as a reason to leave.

"Maybe he never loved me," she said quietly.

Lourdes could hear her cell phone ringing from the living room. She picked herself up and slowly walked down the hall to get it. She found it on the coffee table and she answered it.

"Lourdes…this is Darby…I'm next door. Can you come help me? I think I'm losing my baby?" Darby asked weakly and ended the call.

To be continued…

Text Shan to 22828 to stay up to date with new releases, sneak peeks, contest, and more...
Check your spam if you don't receive an email thanking you for signing up.

Text SPROMANCE to 22828 to stay up to date on new releases, plus get information on contest, sneak peeks, and more!

CPSIA information can be obtained
at www.ICGtesting.com
Printed in the USA
LVHW051531100419
613663LV00017B/784